THE CREW FINDS A LIST

Mabel picked up the list and studied it closely. It was going to be difficult to read with the whole crew watching, especially as the words were faded and all joined up.

Taking a deep breath, Mabel Jones began to read:

"Macaroni."

The captain looked at the crew.

"Does anyone know this varmint that goes by the name MacGroany?"

The crew shook their heads.

The captain banged his fist against the table.

"When I find that treacherous creature MacGroany, I'll rip his head off and throw it to the seagulls!"

The crew cheered.

"Who's next on the list, Mabel?" asked Pelf the goat.

Mabel continued to read:

"Cheddar cheese."

OTHER BOOKS YOU MAY ENJOY

The UNLIKELY ADVENTURES of MABEL JONES

The
UNLIKELY ADVENTURES
of
MABEL JONES

WILL MABBITT
Illustrated by ROSS COLLINS

PUFFIN BOOKS

PUFFIN BOOKS
An imprint of Penguin Random House LLC
375 Hudson Street
New York, New York 10014

First published in the United Kingdom by Puffin,
an imprint of Penguin UK, 2015
Published in the United States of America by Viking,
an imprint of Penguin Young Readers Group, 2015
Published by Puffin Books, an imprint of Penguin Random House LLC, 2016

THE LIBRARY OF CONGRESS HAS CATALOGED THE VIKING EDITION AS FOLLOWS:
Mabbitt, Will.
The unlikely adventures of Mabel Jones / by Will Mabbitt ; illustrated by Ross Collins.
pages cm.—(Mabel Jones ; book 1)
ISBN 978-0-451-47196-3
[1. Pirates—Fiction. 2. Kidnapping—Fiction. 3. Adventure and adventurers—Fiction.]
I. Collins, Ross, illustrator. II. Title.
PZ7.1.M24Un 2015
[Fic]—dc23
2014030543

Designed by Eileen Savage
Printed in the United States of America

Puffin Books ISBN 978-0-14-751425-7

1   3   5   7   9   10   8   6   4   2

For Tilly, Etta, and Ellen

CONTENTS

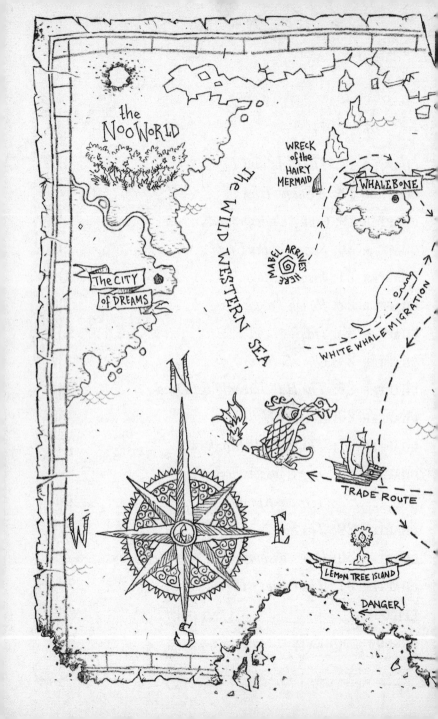

CHAPTER 1
The Kidnap

Mabel Jones was woken by a sudden quiet.
She sat upright.

"What wasn't that noise?" she wondered.

The city outside was strangely soundless.

The neighbors weren't listening to the TV.

The cars weren't driving up and down the busy road.

Even the mice that scuttled under the floorboards observed the eerie silence. A most suspicious silence . . .

Mabel listened very carefully, but even with her eyes closed really tight she couldn't hear where the silence was coming from.

Little did she know that the source of the silence was squeezing through the cat flap with a cutlass in its teeth . . .

. . . tiptoeing through the lounge, leaving wet pawprints on the carpet . . .

. . . creeping up the stairs, pausing for a second to shudder in fear at a photograph of Mabel's great-grandmother . . .

. . . crouching outside Mabel's room with a large, specially designed child-sized sack and, at that very moment, pushing open her bedroom door ready to—

STOP! WAIT!

Before we witness the terrifying sight of young Mabel Jones being skillfully bagged in the dead of night, I believe it is time to reveal the identity of the creature that has invaded her home in such a deafeningly silent fashion.

Let us shine a light into the shadows and reveal the sly beast that lurks in the corner.

Who are you, creature? And what's with the sack?

The creature's whiskers twitch.

Some fur that grows in the wrong direction on top of its head is anxiously straightened with a licked paw.

A pause, then it fixes us with its saucery eyes and blinks nervously, whispering:

"I? I is Omynus Hussh."

It speaks!

And to which species do you belong?

"I is a silent loris."

A dastardly breed: quiet as a peanut and

sneaky as a woodlouse in a jar of raisins.

What brings you to the bedroom of the poor, unfortunate Mabel Jones?

"I is the bagger on board

THE FeROShUS MAggOt!"

The bagger?

"The bagger what bags them children! I gots the proper fingers on me paws that ties the proper knots that keeps the wriggling little snuglet safe inside."

Surely not young Mabel Jones?

"It performed the sacred **DEED. THE DEED** that seals the deal! **THE DEED** that binds it to the captain for a lifetime's service aboard the **Feroshus Maggot**."

The creature leans close and whispers.

"The Deed that shows it's a pirate in the making."

She didn't?

Not **THE DEED?**

"It did! It did! We saws it through the captain's telescope!"

Goodness me! **THE DEED** was performed!

What's that, reader?

You know not of which **DEED** we speak?

Of course not—how silly of me. You probably haven't spent years aboard a pirate ship. You probably haven't ever sat around a fire on a tropical beach finishing the last morsels of a freshly grilled parrot. Then, after the rum has run dry, heard the talk turn to whispered tales of the unfortunate children recruited to piracy after unknowingly performing **THE DEED**!

So let me take you back an hour, to the deck of the pirate ship

THE FeROShUS MAggOt

on which stands one **CAPTAIN IDRYSS EBENEZER SPLIT**.

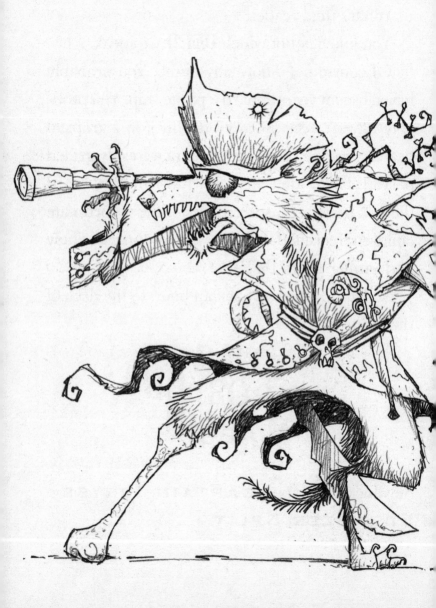

Split is a wolf.

A wolf with a pirate hat and a false leg carved from a human thigh bone. He has a rusty cutlass hanging from his belt and a loaded pistol hidden in his underpants, with no fear of the consequences! His left eye has long since been lost—burned from his skull by a stray firework. His right eye is pressed to the end of a telescope. The telescope is focused on a strange hole in the thick fog that envelops the FeROShUS MAggOt—a hole through which he observes a different world from the one he knows.

A *hooman* world.

A world where young Mabel Jones is about to perform **THE DEED**: the ceremonial picking of Mabel Jones's nose by Mabel Jones's nose-picking finger.

"Has it been eaten yet?" the crew asks eagerly. "Is **THE DEED** complete?"

"Not yet, lads. Not yet!"

Mabel's fate is to be decided by the final destination of the booger currently sitting on her finger. The finger that now pauses precariously between mouth and wall as Mabel makes the decision whether to eat or wipe.

Will she eat it?

Finally she makes the decision. The very same decision that any person believing they were unobserved would make. The same decision being made across the world at this very moment by principals, policemen, lunch ladies, and parents (but especially by principals).

She eats it!

Split allows himself a toothy grin. An extra pair of hands aboard ship could come in useful. At the very least, the child might fetch a modest sum at the next port.

He turns to Omynus Hussh and claps the loris on the back, laughing wickedly.

"Fetch your sack. For tonight you go child-bagging!"

☠

In the bedroom of 23 Gudgeon Avenue, Mabel Jones climbed out of bed to find the source of the suspicious silence.

Looking out of her window, Mabel could see the city was wrapped in thick greeny-gray fog. Only the tops of the tallest tower blocks could be seen.

What an odd night! She wasn't normally woken by a strange quiet. The city wasn't usually—

OUCH!

She had trodden on something.

A peanut!

Why would there be a peanut on her bedroom floor?

I don't even like peanuts, thought Mabel Jones. Apart from the chocolate-covered ones, of course . . . And even then I only like the chocolate part.

Oh! There was another.

And another.

This is strange!

Someone had left a trail of peanuts leading to the darkest corner of her room.

She picked them up one by one.

It's almost as though someone WANTS me to follow them.

Mabel scratched her armpit thoughtfully.

It's almost as though there is somebody in my room.

THERE IS SOMEBODY IN MY ROOM!

Mabel Jones turned to run for the door, but a strong, spindly hand grabbed at her from behind. She opened her mouth to call for help, but only got as far as the "D" in "Dad" before another hand was clamped tightly over her lips and she was wrestled into a sack. Skillful fingers tied a neat knot at the top.

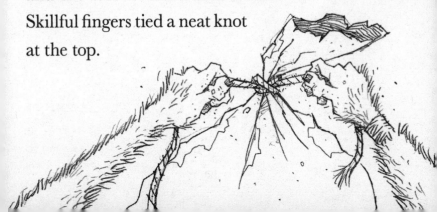

The sack was lifted to the window, where a large pair of hairy arms grabbed it eagerly and pulled it deep into the fog. Then, pausing only to examine a Mabel-Jones-sized bite on his hand, Omynus Hussh climbed up onto the sill and leaped into the night.

Shortly afterward the silence was broken. Above the usual noise of the busy street in the middle of the busy city, far away from the nearest port or shore, the tuneless singing of a rude sea shanty could be heard drifting on the last wisps of the clearing fog.

The neighbors turned up their TVs accordingly.

Chapter 2
Pirates

Mabel Jones was not the sort of girl to be scared of something as silly as being kidnapped by a pirate in the middle of the night.

"My name is Mabel Jones, and I am NOT SCARED of ANYTHING!"

It was dark inside the sack, so she said it again, but louder this time, just to make sure that it was true.

"My name is Mabel Jones, and I am NOT SCARED of ANYTHING!"

Still, she wished her mom or dad was there in the sack with her.

Actually, now she thought about it, it would be better to wish that she *wasn't* here, rather than that her parents *were*. There wasn't enough room in the sack for them, for a start.

Still, they would be worried if she wasn't there when they woke up. Dad always came in to say good-bye before he left for work.

Unseen paws loosened the knot on top of the specially designed child-sized sack, and Mabel Jones climbed out into bright sunshine.

The first thing she noticed after the cawing seagulls and the blinding sun was a severed hand tied to some rope and swinging in the salty breeze.

The last time she had seen those spindly fingers, they had been clamped tightly around her mouth.

14

It turned out that it hadn't taken long for Mabel's bite on Omynus Hussh's paw to go septic.

OLD SAWBONES, the ship's surgeon—an aged and toothless saltwater crocodile—had sighed when he first saw the wound.

"There ain't nothing quite so toxic to a pirate's blood as child spittle mixed with fresh toothpaste . . ."

And, while Omynus Hussh was wondering what "toothpaste" was, Old Sawbones had removed the infected paw with a meat cleaver. There being no spare hooks on board, he had replaced the missing hand with a doorknob.

Omynus Hussh had managed to retrieve the severed hand from Old Sawbones. He planned to keep it in a box for sentimental reasons. But first it needed to be dried. Otherwise it would smell.

"Are ye sure ye really need it?" Old Sawbones had asked, licking his lips.

The second thing Mabel Jones noticed was that she was on board a ship in the middle of the sea. And the ship was crewed by a wild-looking bunch of creatures.

They were all looking at her.

My name is Mabel Jones, and I am NOT SCARED of ANYTHING.

This time she just *thought* it really quietly. She was a bit scared to say it out loud. It was, after all, her first time on a pirate ship.

But I forget myself! You may never have been on a pirate ship either. So let's pause the action on deck and explore the vessel to find out more about its bestial crew.

That door there leads to the captain's cabin. I dare not take you through it, though, for he is still inside.

This open hatch leads below deck.

DOWN
THESE
WOODEN
STEPS...

Careful as you go.

It's dark down here. And damp. This room is where the crew sleeps, in those hammocks slung from the timbers. The smell of sporadic nighttime farting still hangs thick in the air, for the fresh sea breeze does not reach below deck.

That corner is where Old Sawbones works. See his trusty cleaver, its sharpened edge embedded in a wooden block? A certificate in **ADVANCED NAUTICAL SURGERY** from the Butcher's Guild is pinned proudly to the wall.

That there's a crate of ship's biscuits.

Pardon?

Yes, you may try one.

Delicious, no?

Currants? Those are no currants. That's weevil.

Look! The ship's register—the list of names of all the crew on board. It's in the first-aid box, nestled between a half-empty bottle of rum and a box of princess Band-Aids. Let's rejoin the action above deck and put some faces to the names, eh?

Ah! Fresh air. Sunlight!

Right, let's do the roll call.

You already know, of course, the captain: **IDRYSS EBENEZER SPLIT**, a wolf. He has emerged from his cabin to inspect the new arrival. Behind him lurks **Omynus Hussh**, the silent loris. You've met him too. Next comes **OLD SAWBONES**, the saltwater crocodile.

The others you've not met yet . . .

The goat with the pipe is called **PELF**. He's the first mate, all braided beard and grubby fleece.

Then the shiny-faced pig, that's *Milton Melton-Mowbray,* a well-spoken young porker.

The orangutan is **MR. CLUNES**, a strong and silent type.

Not a word has passed his lips for many a moon.

Then you've got the mole, **McMasters**, the best shortsighted lookout ever to have mistaken a pirate ship for an optician's shop.

And that is the crew of the **Feroshus Maggot**, all present and incorrect.

A voice sounds from the top of the mast!

"What is it? I cannae see!" shouted McMasters.

There was muttering and discussion among the crew.

"Tell us what it is, Pelf! What kind of snuglet have we bagged?" asked Milton.

Pelf sucked on his pipe. "A snuglet can come in many shapes, sizes—"

"And flavors!" said Old Sawbones.

"There'll be no eating of the crew *this* voyage, Sawbones. Least not until the biscuits run out." Pelf scratched his impressive horns and blew out a cloud of thick smog. "Aye, but this one is a scrawny lad for sure. A real bag of bones. Not the best type. Not altogether useless, though. A bit short maybe, but he could probably be stretched."

Mr. Clunes cracked his knuckles.

There was a growl from behind the gathered crew.

All eyes turned away from young Mabel Jones and toward the lean and hungry figure that was limping through the crowd: Captain Idryss Ebenezer Split.

His one eye narrowed suspiciously and his lip curled into a snarl, revealing his yellowed fangs.

"Well, well, well . . . What has **THE DEED** brought us this time?"

He grabbed Mabel Jones by the chin and inspected her closely. Very closely indeed.

So closely she could see the rotten meat wedged between his fangs.

His hot wolf-breath crawled all over her face, up inside one nostril, down through the other and then tried to squeeze between her lips.

Mabel coughed politely and hid her nose and mouth beneath her pajama top.

Captain Idryss Ebenezer Split turned to his

crew and uttered an oath so foul it could **NEVER** be written down.

(It contained a word so rude that if an adult whispered it to themselves after bedtime, under the quilt so no one could hear, they could still be arrested and thrown in prison for a very long time.)

The crew huddled together in a worried cuddle as the captain paced the deck. Finally he stopped and, glaring at Mabel Jones, declared in a voice as wicked as a poisoned ice cream:

"This is no boy.
This is a —"

Split gagged. The disgusting word he had reached for caught in his throat like a bad belch.

"This is a —"

He winced. The foulness of the term Split needed left a trail of filth in his mouth as he forced it from his lips.

"This
is
a
GIRL!"

The crew let out a gasp of horror!

"It cannae be!"

"Surely not!"

"A girl?
Girls
can't be
PIRATES!"

"She dids **THE DEED**!"

"She picked her nose . . ."

There was a horrified pause.

". . . and ate it!"

"Girls don't do that . . . do they?"

The crew's eyes fixed upon their captive, young Mabel Jones, who was—just at that moment—absentmindedly picking her nose.

"She's doing it now!"

"I'm just itching!" lied Mabel Jones.

The crew fell into a familiar silence. From the shadows crept the stooped figure of Omynus Hussh, his saucery eyes rimmed with angry tears as he caressed the doorknob at the end of his wrist.

"She's a badlucklet, a filthy smooth no-beard and . . . and a sticky-fingered hand thief!"

Captain Split spat angrily on the deck.

"We'll get no hard work from this prissy little pink princess, and there'll be no passengers aboard my ship! Not this voyage. Not when our treasure is so near!"

He spun around and clomped back to his cabin, shouting:

"TONIGHT SHE WALKS THE GREASY POLE OF CERTAIN DEATH!"

CHAPTER 3
The Greasy Pole of Certain Death

Mabel Jones chewed her lip thoughtfully. She had borrowed a pen and paper from Milton, the pig (who liked to secretly compose *romantic sonnets* in his spare time), and was writing a letter.

Dear Mom,

Hope you'll get this message in a bottle.
It's just a quick note to let you know not to worry about me not being in my bedroom this morning. I've been kidnapped by pirates, who plan to make me walk the Greasy Pole of Certain Death.
Anyway, hope this finds you well.

Love and kisses,
Mabel Jones

p.s. Please don't forget to feed Hamish.
p.p.s. Hamish is the secret pet slug I keep in the shoebox under my bed. He likes to eat Dad's pork pies.
p.p.p.s. He doesn't eat that much, so usually I put the pork pies back in the fridge after he's had a bit, so Dad can still have them in his packed lunch.

I'm not sure if you've ever thrown a message in a bottle over the side of a pirate ship. It's never as easy as it looks.

Often a rogue wave will move the ship just after a bottle has been thrown. This can cause the bottle to smash against the side of the ship, or else return through an open porthole on a lower deck.

One night, a bruised pirate read the note another pirate had accidentally lobbed through his porthole:

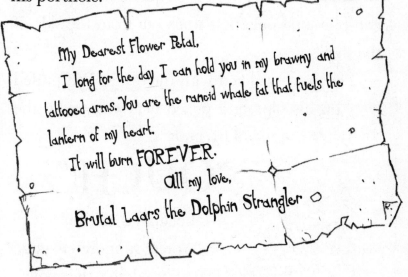

My Dearest Flower Petal,
I long for the day I can hold you in my brawny and tattooed arms. You are the rancid whale fat that fuels the lantern of my heart.
It will burn FOREVER.
All my love,
Brutal Laars the Dolphin Strangler

It was very embarrassing for all concerned.

This time, though, the bottle flew safely overboard. Mabel watched it bob into the distance until it disappeared from sight.

It was getting dark. The shadows grew longer and longer until they crept together into one big dark patch called night.

Mabel Jones stood in her pajamas at the safe end of a long pole that stuck out from the side of the ship.

The crew watched with interest as Pelf puffed on his pipe and poked her gently with the end of his cutlass.

"OUCH!"

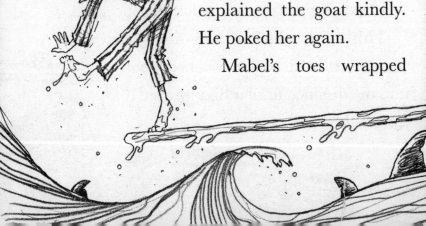

Mabel glared at him.

"You're supposed to edge fearfully along the pole," explained the goat kindly. He poked her again.

Mabel's toes wrapped

around the pole, and bit by bit she edged out to sea. In the light from a swinging lantern, she could see the shapes of large fish swimming alongside the pirate ship.

Sharks? Swordfish? *Killer sardines?*

Mabel gulped.

Things don't look good, she thought.

In fact, they looked about as far away from good as possible. She had almost run out of pole, and her feet were starting to slip.

The pirates looked on expectantly.

"Any final words, girl?" snarled Captain Split.

He made the word "girl" sound like how the smell of **dog poo** would sound if it made a noise.

While we wait for Mabel Jones to

think of something good to say, here are some examples of previous last words that have been uttered before slipping off the Greasy Pole of Certain Death:

"It's actually not that hard to stay standing on this greasy—"

SPLASH!

"Curse you, Captain, and curse your crew. May your pirate souls rot in—"

SPLASH!

And uttered by an unfortunate shipmate:

"Let's grease the pole *before* hanging it over the edge next time, yeah?"

SPLASH!

Mabel, under some pressure to think of something good to say, looked about for inspiration.

From the wrong end of the Greasy Pole of Certain Death, the pirates' ship looked just like you might imagine, like a ship but with added **PIRATEY BITS**. A black flag with a crudely drawn white skull flapped in the breeze. A large, fat **maggot** hung limply from the skull's eye socket. Just below where the Greasy Pole of Certain Death joined the hull was the ship's name. Painted in back-to-front letters, a mix of capitals and low-ercase, it read:

THE ꟻeᴙOShUS MAggoꟑ

"Well, girl?" growled Split. "Anything to say?"

"Yes," said Mabel Jones. "You've spelled the name of your ship wrong. Where it says **Feroshus**."

The crew gasped.

"She can spell!"

"The lassie can read?"

"She's a brainbox!"

Split's good eye narrowed suspiciously.

"And how exactly do you spell **feroshus**?"

Mabel thought hard.

It was a difficult one, that was for sure.

"F . . .

"E . . .

"R . . .

"O . . .

"S . . .

"H . . .

"Erm . . ."

She knew it had an "I" in it somewhere and this was the only place it could fit.

"I . . .

". . . S!"

The crew looked at each other and at the captain.

Split signaled grimly to Pelf. "She's right! Get her back on board! NOW!"

Safely back on the ship, Mabel wiped the grease from her feet.

"Maybe you're not as useless as you look, girl," sneered Split. "Welcome aboard the FeROShUS MAggOt. I've got a little job in mind for you."

Pelf took the pipe from his mouth and put his hoof around Mabel's shoulders.

"Ye be one of us now, Mabel." He looked at her closely. "But we need to make ye look a little more . . . well, a little more piratelike."

"We could remove a leg?" wheezed Old Sawbones. "I'll fetch me cleaver!"

In the end it was decided that, instead of having Old Sawbones amputate a limb, Mabel could wear a belt over her pajamas and, much to her delight, borrow a spare CUTLASS from the hold.

Pelf slapped her on the back.

"Welcome aboard, matey!"

The crew cheered and threw their assorted headgear into the air.

All apart from Omynus Hussh, who stood in a silent sulk, glaring out to sea. An angry teardrop from one of his saucery eyes dripped over the side of the ship and made the water just a tiny bit saltier.

CHAPTER 4
The List

$\mathcal{Y}$esterday morning Mabel Jones had eaten two bowls of cornflakes for breakfast. Then she'd had another one. Then she'd had a slice of toast with strawberry jam for dessert. She'd spread the jam all the way to the edge to make it easier to eat the crusts. Then she'd gone to school.

This morning Mabel Jones had a feeling that she probably wouldn't be going to school.

This morning she was sitting on a barrel in the cabin of a pirate ship, surrounded by a crew of excited animal pirates. It was actually surprisingly similar to being at school except, instead of a nice principal called Mr. Dobson, there was an evil wolf called Captain Idryss Ebenezer Split.

The captain unfolded a piece of paper, and the excited chatter of the crew died down into an expectant silence as he placed it on the table in front of him.

Split turned to Mabel. His muzzle was so

close to her face she could see strings of wet drool between his half-open jaws.

"On this page are written the names of the creatures who stand between me and my destiny. The treacherous bunch of **SCUMBAGS** who stole my rightful inheritance when they mutinied against their captain, my father."

The crew tutted and shook their heads disapprovingly.

Split pulled at the necklace that hung from his neck. Suspended from the rusting chain was a lump of dull black metal.

"Aye! Each one of them has a piece like this, stolen from my poor, dearly departed father."

Pelf leaned in close to Mabel. "It's part of an X!" he whispered.

"A what?" she whispered back.

"**The letter X!** And we all know what the letter X marks, don't we?"

Mabel frowned.

"Do we?" she asked, forgetting to whisper this time.

The captain's lip curled back to reveal purple gums.

"Somewhere, snuglet, somewhere far away, in the **Haunted Seventh Sea**, there is a spot. A spot that's missing its X. I alone knows that spot, and soon I will have all five pieces of the X!"

"But why do you need the X if you already know the spot?" asked Mabel, wrinkling her nose.

Split growled, and his boggled eye boggled even more than usual.

"Because this particular X don't just mark the spot. **It's also a key!**"

"A key?"

"Aye, a key. A key forged in a time long since sunken into the greasy soup of history."

Split pointed to a porthole. "See there! In the sky. **The burning comet!**"

Mabel and the pirates followed his gaze. Sure enough, a little way above the horizon, a light glowed white in the sky. Split traced a path through the air with his cutlass.

"The comet passes just once every hundred years. And while it shines in the sky, if the X is completed and placed correctly, it will unlock a treasure—the most amazing treasure known to beast or hooman."

"Chests of precious jewels!" cried Pelf.

"Piles of golden coins!" croaked Old Sawbones.

"Priceless works of fine art!" squealed Milton Melton-Mowbray.

Captain Split smiled **wickedly**.

"Aye, lads. Something like that . . ."

Pelf removed a star chart from his fleece and unfolded it proudly.

"According to my expert calculations, the comet should—"

"I think you're holding the chart upside-down," said Mabel Jones.

Pelf turned the chart the other way around.

"Aye. According to my calculations, the comet should cross the sky over the next fourteen days."

Captain Split turned to his crew.

"And so we have to gather every piece of the X from the names on this list and reach the spot before the fortnight is out!"

He lovingly smoothed the tattered list with a paw.

"It's been carried across six of the seven seas by bird and by boat"—Split smiled wickedly once more—"but it's never once been read."

The captain's paw shot out and, grabbing Mabel Jones by the collar of her pajamas, he lifted her clean off the ground. His single eye fixed on her as she dangled in the air. She could feel his claws digging into her skin.

"And now we have a reader!"

Split let go of Mabel and she fell to the floor.

"Me?"

"You," he snapped. "So read it!"

Mabel picked up the list and studied it closely. It was going to be difficult to read with the whole crew watching, especially as the words were faded and all joined up.

Taking a deep breath, Mabel Jones began to read:

"Macaroni."

The captain looked at the crew.

"Does anyone know this varmint that goes by the name MacGroany?"

The crew shook their heads.

The captain banged his fist against the table.

"When I find that treacherous creature MacGroany, I'll rip his head off and throw it to the seagulls!"

The crew cheered.

"Who's next on the list, Mabel?" asked Pelf the goat.

Mabel continued to read:

"Cheddar cheese."

The crew looked at each other again, shaking their heads. He wasn't a pirate they were familiar with either.

"I'll tie him to a carnivorous squid!" cried the captain, snapping a chair in half.

Mabel continued reading the list:

"Mustard."

"So ferocious he's known by a single name!" gasped Old Sawbones.

"I'll stuff him like a mackerel," whispered the captain, curling his lip to reveal his razor-sharp teeth.

The crew winced.

Mabel looked at the captain politely. "Shall I finish?"

The last item was written in a different handwriting.

"Lemon juice," read Mabel.

"Lemon Juice?"

The crew looked at one another in confusion.

Finally Pelf spoke. "It's just a shopping list, isn't it?"

"Yes, I think so." Mabel smiled apologetically at the crew.

The captain's single eye boggled with rage. Throwing back his head, he howled the

loudest howl

ever heard by man or beast. He drew his cutlass and swung it angrily through the air, twisting it into the heart of an imaginary enemy. Then he turned to point it at Mabel.

"Then I guess that makes you pretty useless, snuglet!"

Omynus Hussh appeared from the shadows.

"Slice her open, Captain! She's made you look like a fool!"

But Mabel wasn't even listening. She was thinking.

Something wasn't quite right . . .

Somewhere deep inside her head a thought was waking up and scratching itself.

Why is the last item written by a different hand?

Then that thought rudely poked a new thought awake with a bony finger.

And why would you need lemon juice in what is obviously a recipe for macaroni and cheese?

Lemon juice?

Lemon juice . . .

Lemon. Juice.

LEMON JUICE!

Spinning away from the captain's sword, Mabel Jones held the list above a candle.

"Go on, burns it!" scoffed Omynus Hussh. "It's as worthless as a girl on a pirate ship."

"I'm not burning it. Just look!" cried Mabel.

The crew gasped as they looked at the list. Below the recipe for macaroni and cheese, new words were forming—and this time they were names.

"Invisible ink!" declared Mabel proudly. "The heat from the flame turns the invisible words written in lemon juice brown!"

The crew burst into applause.

"The girl's a marvel!"

"A brainbox!"

"Who'd have thought it?!"

Mabel placed the list on the table and the crew gathered around as she began to read:

"The Mutineers of *The Flying Slug*: Bartok the Brute."

Now wait a second while I find my *Who's Who of Pirates* sticker album. Yes, it is complete, apart from a sticker of **"Elusive" Jack Carrot, the Rabbit Assassin**. No one has ever managed to collect that sticker. (If you find it, please send it to the address in the back of this book. I can swap **Eric the Tuneless Canary** and **"Strangling" Hans Van Snood, the Murderous Gerbil of Ghent** for it.)

Ah, here he is. Page 7.

PANUNI'S
Who's Who of PIRATES
83   83

BARTOK the BRUTE

AKA: THE BEAST OF THE BALTIC

⚓ Achievements of note ⚓

① The sinking of a submarine by punching it in the hull

② The sinking of an ironclad by punching it in the hull

③ The sinking of a tramp steamer by ... well, you get the picture

Mabel continues:

"Ishmael H. Toucan."

Found him! Under the subsection "Former Pirates," for his fortune was made as a whaler of the *Cold Gray Sea*. He shares his entry with his brother, **Abel**, and holds records for both harpooning and whale butchery.

"The passenger, **Count Anselmo Klack**."

No entry for the count. I guess he is not a real pirate. He is a count, though, which is a mark of badness if ever I saw one.

'Old Hoss.'

Ah, Old Hoss the sheep! I know him well. And so does Captain Split, for Old Hoss carved the captain's bone leg. Here's his sticker in the "Smuggling and Thievery" section! A dastardly sheep who would steal from his own mother if he hadn't already pushed her off a cliff.

The captain flashed a wicked fanged grin and addressed the happy crew.

"All hands on deck, boys! Today we sail and tomorrow . . . tomorrow we steal!"

Mabel looked up.

"So can I go home now, please?"

Split laughed a nasty laugh.

"There ain't no way home for you, snuglet. When a hooman child commits **THE DEED**, it opens a porthole between your world and ours, so we pirates can go through and bag 'em. But once we've snatched the wriggling snuglet and come back through the porthole, **then it closes behind us**."

Mabel gulped. "You mean I'm trapped here . . . forever?"

Split leaned in close to her, his hot wolf-breath stinking up all her face holes at once.

"Well, now that you mention it, there is one way back. Remember how I told you the **X** is a key?"

Mabel nodded.

"Well, one of the things that key can open is a

porthole back to the hooman world. So here's the deal: if you help us find them missing bits of X, then maybe, when I've got *my* treasure, I'll open a porthole that will take you back home."

Split grinned an evil grin.

"Meantime fear not, snuglet . . . I'll look after you . . ."

CHAPTER 5
The Cadaverous Lobster Tavern

Once on the shore of the **WILD WESTERN SEA**, head up the stony beach along from the wreck of the *Hairy Mermaid* and you will find the town of Whalebone.

Ignore the tired gaze of the jaded old mariner on the seafront and scuttle past the dark alley where the dogs of the sea toss seal knuckles against the wall of the jail.

Turn right at the mackerel steamers, then left past **DIRTY SIMON'S TATTOO AND TANNING**

SALON and you will see, directly in front of you, the studded oak door of the **CADAVEROUS LOBSTER TAVERN.**

Mabel brushed some snow from the guidebook she was reading. Sure enough, the **CADAVEROUS LOBSTER TAVERN** lay in her path. She didn't know what 'cadaverous' meant, but, from the look of the lobster on the creaking sign, it wasn't a compliment.

But wait!

What brings a young girl to a place such as this? Mabel Jones, though brave of heart, is hardly the sort you'd usually find in a pub. And this is not the sort of pub where children are greeted by a friendly face, a pint of rum, and an arm-wrestle. This is not the kind of pub where a rosy-nosed barmaid welcomes strangers with a kiss on the cheek and a whale-fat sandwich.

No, this pub is the haunt of the roughest of all seagoing folk. Where wild-eyed animals fight over the last scraps of stolen treasure; where knives are drawn over spilled drinks; where those who can't pay their bills are held down and forcibly tattooed.

But young Mabel Jones is here on a mission. A mission to find the owner of the first name on the list and rob, pinch, or pilfer their piece of the shattered X.

Oh, it's OK. Here come some others, tramping through the snow.

It appears she is in the responsible company of a couple of bloodthirsty pirates. The perfect partners for a nighttime stroll to the roughest pub in the toughest town in the northern hemisphere.

A meeting had been held on board the **Feroshus Maggot** and the three pirates chosen to steal the piece of X were Pelf, Mr. Clunes, and young Mabel Jones.

You might wonder if Mabel was an odd choice for the mission, considering she wasn't really old enough to go into a pub late at night. And you'd be right to wonder. Something tells me the whispered, wicked voice of one Omynus Hussh must have been employed to drip poisoned words like runny honey into the captain's ear.

"Mabel should go pinch it from hims too! Prove the snuglet is loyal to you, Captain. Prove she's a **pirate**!"

And speaking of Omynus Hussh . . . who's that lurking in the shadows, unseen by the official landing party?

One more pirate!

A pirate who snuck off after them, scuttling some yards behind. Always watching. Always in the shadows. Shrouded in a suspicious silence, his large, saucery eyes rimmed with angry tears.

He lifts a severed, air-dried hand from beneath his shirt and holds it against his cheek as though it were the softest of kittens.

"We'll gets her good and proper this time. We'll gets her good and proper . . ."

Maybe it would be best if we skipped the rest of this chapter. I wish I could tell you that it would all end happily, but the truth is things are about to get **very unpleasant** for poor Mabel Jones . . .

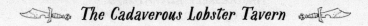

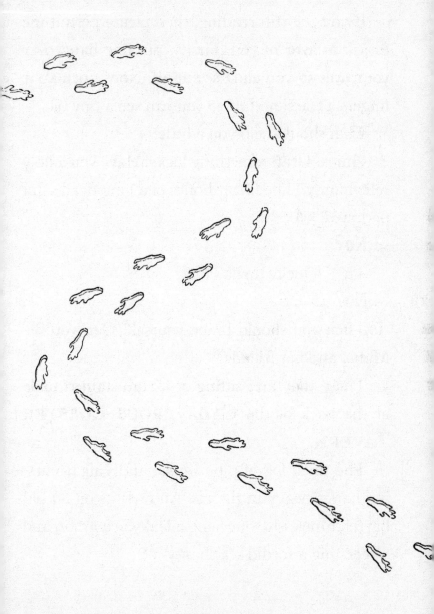

If you are still reading, then please permit me to ask a favor of you. Firstly, put one hand over your eyes so you can't see at all. Now, open your fingers a fraction. Just so you can see a tiny bit.

That should help you a little.

Quick! Grab something lucky. Have you a holy relic handy? The finger bones of a long-dead saint perhaps?

No?

Then a lucky turtle's foot?

No?

Then you should brace yourself. Can you see Mabel and her friends?

There they are: sitting at a rum-stained table at the back of the **CADAVEROUS LOBSTER TAVERN**.

The thick fog of pipe smoke and vulgar cursing hangs heavy in the air. An owl sits on an old barrel, tunelessly squeezing a leaky accordion and screeching a sordid sea shanty.

It's been a while since I have visited this place (due to an unfortunate incident with an octopus beak and several members of the Alsatian Navy). It hasn't changed much, though.

The floor is still covered in sawdust to soak up

spilled drinks and spilled blood. The picture of the landlord's late wife still hangs threateningly over the bar beneath a **blunderbuss** kept loaded for closing time. The tables are still pieced together from driftwood, and the old goat, Slops, is still asleep in the corner, racked by nightmares from his time at sea. His lips mouth the same words he uttered on that fateful voyage when he contracted the **Tropical Bumrot** that curses him still:

"It must've been something I ate . . ."

But enough description of this foul house for the toughest and roughest of the sea. Let us quickly peek over Mabel's shoulder to remind ourselves of the first name on the list. The owner of the name sits just there, at that table by the bar. The wild and wicked and willfully evil

BARTOK THE BRUTE,
THE BEAST OF THE BALTIC!

And what a beast!

Bartok the Brute is a bear.

A bear covered from head to paw in wiry black hair that conceals tattoos so rude they'd make a dock worker blush. He has shoulders so wide he has to edge sideways through doors, and claws as white as the cow bones he cracks open with his very, very large teeth. It is rumored he once suffered a direct hit to the head from a cannonball. The only damage: a bloodied snout. Somewhere—set deep into his face—are tiny, tiny eyes like burned currants on an overcooked cake. And around his neck hangs a dull metal shard: one piece of an ancient letter **X**.

Mabel looked across at the crowd of pirates gathered around Bartok's table as they let out a rowdy cheer.

"What are they doing?" she asked.

Pelf looked disapprovingly at the pirates.

"It's a drinking competition. This tavern is famous for its home-brewed **Wasp Rot**. They each drink a shot in turn and the first pirate to fall down loses."

"Wasp Rot? What's Wasp Rot?" asked Mabel. Pelf screwed his face up.

"A foul liquid brewed from the pee of a thousand stray cats and laced with crushed wasp. Only those with innards like the bowels of hell can drink it in any amount! A little bit will knock you senseless. A little more will dissolve you from the inside out. A smooth-faced young snuglet like you? It would kill you dead—but not before you got the **brain rot** and your eyes fell backward into the empty space left behind."

Mabel winced. "*You* don't drink it, do you?"

Pelf took a big suck of his foul-smelling pipe and coughed out a toxic cloud of gray-green smoke. He cleared his throat and spat the contents onto the sawdusty floor.

"Not me. That poison will kill you. My body's a temple!"

He nodded his head toward the table, where a gray-whiskered hound was being carried away, unconscious. Another victory for Bartok the Brute!

A large paw banged on the table, and Bartok's voice boomed out:

"BARTOK PLAY AGAIN!"

The owl stopped squeezing the accordion. The crowd fell silent. Everyone looked at each other shiftily. It was clear that this was one game it was more fun to watch than to play.

"BARTOK IS WAITING!"

Would no one dare challenge the Beast?

"BARTOK IS ANGRY!"

Suddenly the silence was broken—by a familiar voice from an unseen mouth. Words spoken through treacherous loris lips:

"I thinks the thieving snuglet-in-the-corner should play."

The crowd parted from Bartok's table. All eyes, noses, beaks, and muzzles turned to Mabel Jones and her friends.

"BARTOK DRINK WITH SCRAWNY ONE!"

Mabel looked around innocently.

"Who? Me?"

The crowd broke into cheering. A challenger had been found! The owl restarted his shanty and Mabel was carried, protesting, to the table.

"BARTOK WANT BET!"

Pelf tapped his pipe against a hoof thoughtfully.

"I bet you the piece of X hanging from your neck that Mabel will win!"

Mabel looked at Pelf in horror.

Pelf winked back at her. "Worth a shot, matey, as you've volunteered anyway."

Once more the crowd fell into silence as Bartok considered the bet.

"WHAT DOES BARTOK WIN?"

The whispery voice spoke again from the shadows with treacherous, betraying words:

"If you wins, you can keep the whole child!"

Mabel gasped. It was all happening so quickly! Just as she was about to protest one decision, another much worse one was being made.

Bartok looked at her closely.

"BARTOK ACCEPT. BARTOK HUNGRY!"

The Beast lifted a giant paw toward the bottle of **Wasp Rot** on the table, but, before he could pour, a bar stoat leaned forward.

"The challenger chooses the drink, remember?"

He jumped back into the crowd as the Beast glared at him.

"NO MATTER. BARTOK DRINK ANYTHING."

He glared at Mabel.

"CHOOSE!"

"Can I see a drinks menu?"

The stoat scratched his stomach.

"We have **Wasp Rot** and **Diet Wasp Rot**."

"Do they both have cat pee in them?"

The stoat nodded.

"And you haven't got anything else?" Mabel asked.

The stoat shook his head.

"Haven't you even got any water?"

The pirates laughed. "The only thing water is good for is carrying a ship full of **Wasp Rot**!"

"Lemonade?"

The pirates guffawed wildly. The very thought: pirates drinking lemonade?

"Orange squash!?"

More laughter. They hadn't even heard of orange squash. It just sounded funny!

"Milk?"

The bar fell into a horrified silence.

Milk?!

MILK?!?

MILK?!?!

The pirates cowered from the table.

Pelf pushed through the crowd and grabbed Mabel by the collar of her pajamas.

"Are ye mad? Are ye insane? It'll rot your teeth straight from your gums and make your bones crumble like a ship's biscuit. Many a fine pirate has got the screaming fever just by sniffing that filthy stuff. You can't drink milk! It just ain't right. It's . . . it's . . .

"DISGUSTING!"

I'm afraid we must pause the story for an important health and safety announcement. I am not sure where a creature like you comes from, or indeed if you have even heard of this "milk," so let me explain. This vile, white filth that squirts from the teat of a cow is avoided by all but the maddest of pirate folk. It tastes all . . . all . . . clean . . . and creamy . . . and cold. With milk, there is no acrid aftertaste, no burned flavor, no throat burning. It is best avoided. And if anyone should offer it to you, then you should throw it back in their face on account of them being a dirty, rotten poisoner. I urge you NEVER, NEVER, EVER choose the Devil's Drink, also known as milk. And this was the drink that Mabel chose!

Poor young Mabel Jones. She couldn't possibly have known. (I told you this chapter would be too much for you!)

The bar stoat gingerly placed two glasses of milk on the table, then retreated to a safe distance.

"DRINK! DRINK! DRINK!" chanted the pirates from their respective hiding-places.

Bartok raised the drink to his lips.

Mabel did the same.

"DRINK! DRINK! DRINK!"

Their gazes locked together.

"DRINK!

DRINK!

DRINK!"

Mabel gulped her milk down in one go and . . .

. . . and . . .

. . . and smiled!

SHE SMILED!

A triumphant, milky mustache on her top lip.

In Bartok's tiny burned-currant eyes, Mabel saw a flash of fear—just for a second—and then they were blazing with an angry fire once again. Bartok began to drink, but with the first swallow there came a muted belch from somewhere deep inside his hairy body. Mabel winced as milk started to spray from his nostrils.

Bartok grabbed the table for support, but it was

no good. The vile liquid was taking hold of his body, its goodness suffocating his essential pirate organs. Gargling in pain, he collapsed to the floor.

"BARTOK FEEL POORLY."

His eyes flickered closed and then, a second later, he let out a loud snore.

THE BEAST
WAS DEFEATED!

The pirate crowd cheered as Pelf leaned down and removed the piece of X from around Bartok's neck. Ducking through the excited crowd, the landing party from the **Feroshus Maggot** excused themselves and were heading for the door when . . .

A hand grabbed Mabel by the pajamas.

A small, soft hand, very much like her own, belonging to a very tall, very thin hooded figure, very much *un*like her.

Mabel looked up and, for a split second, the

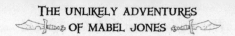

clouds cleared, and the moonlight shone through the grubby windows of the tavern, revealing the face of the mysterious figure.

IT WAS A SKULL!

A skull! All white bone and hollow, dead holes where eyes should be.

Mabel stared at the bone face, wanting to turn away from its no-eyed glare. But realizing that would be rude, and might even hurt the creature's feelings, she forced herself to look it straight in the eye holes.

A soft voice spoke from deep within the creature's chest, its jawbone moving up and down, weirdly out of time with the words:

"What are you doing with that piece of X?"

Mabel blinked. "I'm collecting the pieces for Captain Idryss Ebenezer Split. If I help him find them all, he can use them to send me home."

She tried to pull away, but the creature held her firmly by the sleeve.

"You mustn't help Split," it hissed urgently. "If he gets hold of all five pieces, he—"

"Mabel?"

It was Pelf speaking, coming back to see why she hadn't followed the others out.

The tall creature took one look at the goat, then pressed a card into Mabel Jones's hand and disappeared into the crowded pub.

Mabel looked at the card.

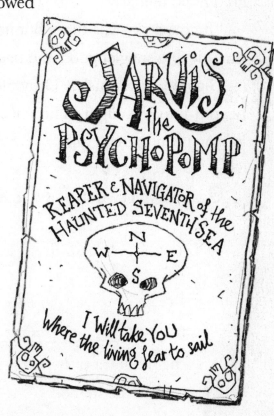

JARVIS the PSYCHOPOMP

REAPER & NAVIGATOR of the HAUNTED SEVENTH SEA

N W E S

I will take YOU where the living fear to sail

And with that last, most mysterious encounter, and the second piece of the X safely in hand, the pirates left the CADAVEROUS LOBSTER TAVERN.

All but one, that is: a saucer-eyed silent loris, consoling himself in the corner. He kissed his severed hand tenderly.

"It gots lucky this time. But next time we'll get the thieving snuglet good and nasty!"

Giggling nervously, Omynus Hussh disappeared into the night. The only clue to his ever having been there at all?

a suspicious silence.

CHAPTER 6
A Storm and Some Filthsome Treachery

*A*h, what a life it is to be a pirate! It's a tough one, surely. Creatures like Mabel Jones are not used to the harsh ways of the sea, being more at ease safely snuggled in their feathery beds. And it is also true that her puny arms could not heave an anchor or even lift a cannonball, but still she applied herself to her new life with a vigor that surprised the pirate crew.

Mabel now knew the only way of returning

home was to help the pirates complete their mission.

But the Psychopomp's words bounced and buzzed about her brain like a gang of drunken mosquitoes looking for a fight.

"You mustn't help Split."

Without knowing why she mustn't, Mabel could only focus on what she *did* know—she needed that X. And another part of the X was now their target. The part belonging to the captain of a whaling vessel. His name: **Ishmael H. Toucan.**

The Logbook of
Capt. Ishmael H. Toucan

Call me Ishmael.

I am the captain of the Peapod, currently lying 68 degrees north-northwest, in the coldest corner of the Cold Gray Sea.

This is the last entry in the captain's log.

Four years at sea and still no sign of the blasted white whale that consumed my only brother, Abel.

Oh Abel, if you were here it would fill my heart with joy! But perhaps it is good that you are not, for now the very seas have started to plot against us. The moon taunts us from the safety of the sky and the wind laughs a shrieking laugh as it sweeps across the deck. Our ship, the Peapod, lies caught between two giant, frozen ice floes and threatens to splinter at any moment.

I fear for the ship but not for myself, for without you life is as empty as the ship's hold. Alas, no whale has been harpooned since our argument on that fateful day.

Oh, if only I'd allowed you that last piece of cheesecake, even though, as the eldest brother, it was rightfully mine!

Oh, if only you had not taken the cheesecake anyway and made off in the rowing boat to eat it in peace!

Oh, if only at that exact moment, a giant white whale hadn't risen from the depths and swallowed you, the boat, and the slice of cheesecake whole . . .

Life has been cruel to us, Abel, but I would not curse my fate if I had been given just one last chance to say to you:

"Abel, Abel my brother, I love thee . . ."

And maybe add:

"You owe me a slice of cheesecake."

Then I would die a happy toucan.

Signed,

Ishmael H. Toucan

Captain of the Peapod

Sad words indeed! And a coincidence too, for at the very moment Captain Ishmael H. Toucan was scribbling his signature, his name was being read out from a list of particular interest to *another* captain, one Idryss Ebenezer Split.

"**Ishmael H. Toucan**," read Mabel.

Enraged by the very name, Split hurled his half-empty tankard at Milton, the pig, and struck him full in the snout.

"Ishmael the whaler!" he growled. "I know that sell-out well! Turned his back on piracy for a lucrative career in whaling!"

He stabbed a rusty dagger into a map spread across his cabin table. "Set sail for the *Cold Gray Sea*!"

If the crew had thought that recovering the first piece of the X from Bartok the Brute would put the captain in a kinder mood, they were very much mistaken.

In fact, the only thing that matched the captain's rage was the sea. As the days passed, the captain grew angrier and angrier and, with each cruel punishment handed out to his unfortunate crew, the waves grew ever higher.

The freezing north winds **LASHED** the pirates as they went about their business. Milton had lent Mabel an oilskin that she buttoned up right to her nose. Two sealskin boots and some mittens completed her outfit, but it was still cold enough to freeze the snot that dripped from her runny nose.

At night the crew huddled together below, the long arms of Mr. Clunes circling the shivering group. Only Split stayed on deck, constantly surveying the horizon through his telescope, watching as the comet slowly crossed the starry sky.

One morning, Mabel rose early. Captain Split had finally retired to his cabin, and Pelf was standing at the helm, looking out to sea with a worried frown.

He extinguished his pipe and tucked it safely into his grubby fleece.

"ALL HANDS ON DECK!"

Pelf stamped a hoof to wake those that slept below. "There be an evil storm brewing."

Mabel followed his concerned gaze. Sure enough, terrible black clouds were gathering on the horizon.

Pelf pulled his beard thoughtfully. "Drop anchor, Mr. Clunes. We'll stay here until the storm has passed us by."

Clunes, the silent orangutan, began to lower the anchor. He was the only one on board strong enough to lift it, but Clunes's face showed no sign of strain as he raised the giant weight. His expression stayed the same as it always was: sad.

A fierce voice sounded from the doorway of the captain's cabin.

"Weigh anchor, Mr. Clunes!"

It was the captain. His mad eye boggled with rage. "Captain Idryss Ebenezer Split stops for no storm!"

Pelf held tightly to the rail as another large wave rocked the boat.

"But there's a tornado coming, Captain!" he shouted through the howling wind.

The captain's one eye swiveled and fixed Pelf with a terrible stare.

"Didn't mean to question, sir," said Pelf. "Weigh anchor. Steer a course for straight ahead!"

Had Pelf known the fury of the storm to come, he might have disobeyed the orders and faced the captain's rage instead. For the sea grew rougher and rougher, and the **Feroshus Maggot** pitched and rolled with each wave as though it was a toy boat.

Then a giant wave, bigger than any that had come before, swept the deck of the ship. All but McMasters in the crow's nest were covered by water. Just before the ship was swamped, Mabel heard his voice calling:

"Och! I think there's a storm heading this way!"

Mabel felt a stab of panic as she was swept off her feet and squashed against the side rail. Looking over, she could see that the ship was perched atop a

huge cliff of angry, swirling water. In a second, it dropped with stomach-turning speed so that it was at the bottom of a new cliff that threatened to collapse on top of them.

From her position wedged in the rail, she saw Milton Melton-Mowbray washed overboard by a great wave—apparently lost forever—only to be deposited back on deck with a **bump** as another wave crashed into the ship.

Some of the crew had tied themselves to masts. Others, like Mabel, were clinging to anything fixed to the deck. It was a funny time for Mabel to notice something relatively small and pointless. She only noticed it because it seemed so . . .

. . . so *odd*.

It was a footprint on the deck beside her. A hooman footprint! Someone had trod cannon grease across the deck.

Could it be my footprint?

Mabel looked more closely. Whoever had made the footprint had much smaller feet than her. And they hadn't been wearing sealskin boots.

How strange!

Then the thought popped from her brain as another huge wave—this time port side—struck the **Feroshus Maggot**. The force popped Mabel free from the rails. Mr. Clunes's strong and hairy hands grabbed her as she slid across the deck, and the pair braced themselves for the next wave, one that would surely break the ship in two.

But it
didn't come.

Seconds passed.

The sea was calm.

Dead calm.

Milton looked out from under an upturned barrel. "I say, what's happened to the waves?"

Captain Split gazed into the distance.

"We be in the eye of the storm! The ship will be struck again as we pass through the other side." He looked around at the crew. "Lash yerselves fast. I won't find the next piece of the X if ye scurvy scum be washed overboard."

And with that he stomped back to his cabin, clipping Milton behind the ear with a smart blow from his paw.

Mabel looked out to sea. Sure enough, in the distance the waves were stormy and black, but around the **Feroshus Maggot** the waters were so calm that it looked as though they were sailing in a freshly poured bath. She leaned over the side, her tiptoes just scraping the deck.

"It's so clear!"

A school of fish passed underneath the boat. Different colors, all darting among each other, forming an ever-changing, living rainbow.

Mabel Jones leaned over further still as the last one disappeared from view. "It's so *beautiful*!"

She felt a doorknob-shaped prod to her bottom.

Then
she
was
falling.
Falling?
FALLING OVERBOARD!

A silent shadow moved away from the spot where Mabel had lost her balance.

Sometimes the quietest actions achieve the greatest results, and all it had taken was a whisper of a push from a doorknob attached to the arm of a silent loris to send Mabel tumbling over the side.

She heard a voice shouting:

"Snuglet overboard!"

And then, with a terrible splash, Mabel Jones plunged into the freezing depths of the *Cold Gray Sea*.

CHAPTER 7
That Sinking Feeling

Sinking . . .

Sinking . . .

Sinking . . .

Sinking . . .

Down here the water was clear as a stolen crystal. Deep below, large formations of rock projected from the seabed, almost like giant buildings, neatly separated from one another by criss-crossing roads.

As the currents buffeted her back and forth, for a second Mabel almost believed she was flying high above the streets of an underwater city.

Curious, that it all seemed so . . .

Well . . . so familiar.

Maybe she was dreaming?

She closed her eyes.

For a second she was back at home in her bedroom.

"MOM?" she called. "DAD?!"

Then the freezing briny water of the *Cold Gray Sea* filled her mouth and she choked awake with the realization:

I'm drowning!

A shape approached. Or was this still a dream?

A huge, pale shape with a smaller, darker, mouth-shaped shadow at the front.

It's coming nearer.

Now the smaller, darker, mouth-shaped shadow was **huge**, and the **huge**, pale shape was

enormous.

Nearer and nearer . . .

And now Mabel could see the huge, darker, mouth-shaped shadow was lined with thousands of tiny teeth, and between those teeth danced tiny fish.

This is a strange dream.

And then she realized the tiny teeth weren't as tiny as she thought. They were more the size of fingers. **Big fingers.**

And then the coldness was replaced by darkness and she couldn't see anything at all . . .

Oh, Mabel.

Poor young Mabel Jones.

Pass me that handkerchief so I may dry my eyes.

Poor, sweet, kindly, innocent, nose-picking Mabel Jones. Taken from us by the wickedest deed of Omynus Hussh, the Silent Assassin—his natural goodness blinded by the angry tears of misplaced rage.

Strap me down, friend. Prepare the tattooing needle.

Or, if you don't have the nerve or a steady hand, phone **DIRTY SIMON'S TATTOO AND TANNING SALON** and book me a lunchtime slot.

For Mabel must be remembered—her name tattooed across the left cheek of my bottom.

Aye, it will need to be carefully shaved first.

MABEL JONES, R.I.P.

And now etch her face upon my right buttock.

Thank you.

A fine job!

Aye, it's still a little sore but it will heal. Now poor Mabel Jones will be remembered whenever I need to scratch my bum in public.

What's that?

You feel she might still be alive?!

YOU REALLY THINK SO?!

Quick, then. Fetch me a soft cushion and let's continue with the story. Let us pray to Neptune that something, anything, has saved her from a freezing watery grave!

Well?

What are you waiting for?

TURN

THE

PAGE!

CHAPTER 8
The Unremitting Drip

Drip

Drip

Drip

Drip

Drip Drip

Drip Drip

Drip

DripDripDrip

Drip

CHAPTER 9
Mabel Escapes
the Unremitting Drip

*M*abel moved her head sleepily to avoid the water that was drip-drip-dripping on her forehead. It had begun to get quite annoying.

Then she sat up, wide awake, and smiled.

It was a smile as big as when you wake up expecting to go to school but then remember it's the first day of summer vacation. Except this smile was even bigger, because she'd woken up expecting to be dead but then realized she wasn't.

"I'M ALIVE!"
ALIVE
ALIVE
ALIVE

"Oooh, there's an echo!"

echo

echo

echo

It was so dark Mabel had to gently feel her eyeballs to make sure she hadn't forgotten to open her eyes.

Wet slimy walls +
water lapping at ankles
= a cave

"That explains the echo!"

echo

echo

echo

She couldn't see the other side of the cave or an entrance of any sort, but a tiny beam of light shone through a small hole several yards above her head. The cave was ankle-deep in water. Mabel had woken up half in and half out of it. (Her pajamas were soaking.) All around the cave, as far as she could see, was flotsam and jetsam—the miscellaneous rubbish of the sea. Driftwood, old barrels, parts of ships. Even some unopened crates.

Suddenly the cave was flooded with light. An entrance had opened, letting in a rush of water that lapped around her knees. The newly opened entrance was lined with pointed stalactites and stalagmites, which looked remarkably like sharp teeth—a bit like the mouth of a huge animal.

"It's just like I'm inside the stomach of a huge whale and am looking out of its mouth," said Mabel Jones.

"Oh! I *am* inside a huge whale and looking out of its mouth!"

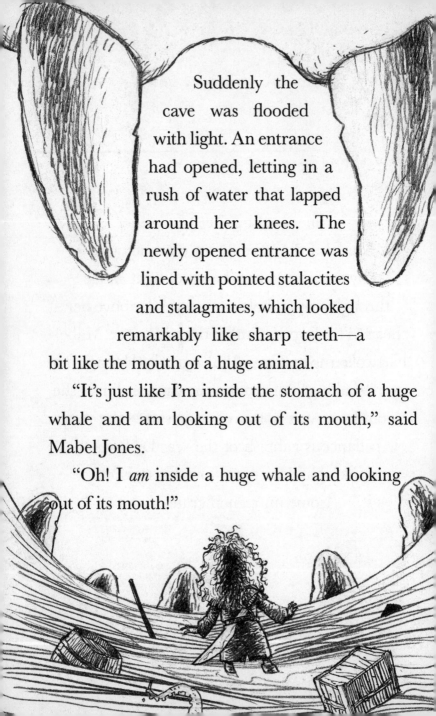

Then the mouth closed again. But now the insides of the whale were lit with the soft glow of a very large, freshly swallowed luminescent jellyfish.

Mabel sat down to think.

"I wonder how long it takes to be digested by a whale?"

Mabel jumped as a sad voice answered:

"It seems to take quite some time, I'm afraid."

Mabel hadn't noticed that she was sitting next to a rather dejected-looking toucan.

"My name is Abel H. Toucan," he said, offering Mabel a wing tip to shake. "Welcome to my home and my prison for four long years. I'm afraid there is no way out. The only hope is to sit and pray that the whale eventually beaches itself."

Mabel frowned.

She didn't have time to hang about. She needed to get back to the **Feroshus Maggot**. With every hour that passed, the comet was crossing the sky. And if the pieces of the X weren't all found by the time it disappeared, she'd be stuck in this world forever. The life of a pirate wasn't all bad—she glanced fondly at her cutlass—but she did want to get home. And, if she couldn't get out of this whale, she would never see her mom and dad again . . .

Mabel Jones bit her lip.

PIRATES.

DON'T.

CRY.

She'd have plenty of time to cry once she was safely home.

She looked around the whale's innards. An old

rowing boat was tied to a giant rib. On the boat, Abel had built a small shack of driftwood and seaweed. Useful items swallowed by the whale had been carefully stored in a pile at the back.

"I think you've made it rather nice," she said thoughtfully.

The toucan smiled a sad smile.

"Ah, but all the comforts in the world can't replace the love of a family or the cuddle of a sibling."

Mabel nodded. She knew what it was like to miss your family.

Abel H. Toucan held up an angry fist of feathers to the sky (or, rather, to where the sky would be if they weren't inside the stomach of a whale several fathoms underwater).

"Oh, Ishmael! Oh, my brother! Were it not for this accursed whale, we should be together!"

He fixed Mabel with a crazed stare.

"Our last words were in anger! It pains me that

he might remember me unkindly, for although that last slice of cheesecake was rightfully mine (me being the younger brother) I should at least have let him have a bit."

For it was (if you had not already guessed) the brother of Ishmael H. Toucan with whom Mabel now chatted inside the atmospherically lit bowels of the fabled White Whale of the *Cold Gray Sea*.

Abel's crazed look was replaced with a kindly smile.

"But I forget myself and my manners. Do you like lemonade?"

Mabel nodded. She was rather thirsty.

"The other day the whale swallowed a hundred barrels of the stuff. I can't abide it. It gives me terrible wind"—Abel lowered his voice to a polite whisper—"and makes me suffer the foulest of belches, for my diet has been a trifle ripe in fish of late."

But Mabel didn't reply. A tiny spark of imagination had lit up her brain and was beginning to smolder like the fuse of a cannon. It was a risky idea for sure, and if it backfired . . .

Well, if it backfired it meant . . .

CERTAIN DEATH!

CHAPTER 10
The Fish Burps

Call me Ishmael.

I am the captain of the Peapod, currently lying 68 degrees north-northwest in the coldest corner of the Cold Gray Sea.

This is definitely the last entry in the captain's log, for pirates have boarded my stricken vessel and she is ablaze. They want my piece of X, but they shall not have it. For if they come any closer, I shall drop it into this hole in the ice and it will be lost forever in the freezing depths.

Like Abel! Oh, Abel! How I miss thee!

Your beloved brother,

Ishmael

The pirates, led by the ferocious Captain Idryss Ebenezer Split, paused in their advance across the deck of the **PEAPOD**.

Captain Split's plan had been going swimmingly. Luckily for the pirates, the storm-battered **Feroshus Maggot** had been deposited by the tornado in an area of clear water within sight of the **PEAPOD**. The pirates, still mourning the loss of their beloved crewmate Mabel Jones, had launched an immediate assault across the ice. Silently, cutlasses in gritted teeth, they had climbed unnoticed aboard the stricken **PEAPOD**.

Unnoticed that is until Milton Melton-Mowbray knocked over a lantern with a stray trotter.

"Oh, I say—what rotten luck!"

The burning whale fat had set the **PEAPOD**'s sail and Pelf's fleece ablaze. It had taken a dunking in a barrel of pickled onions to extinguish the flames. Pelf's screams and the smell of vinegary goat had woken Captain Ishmael.

Now the ship was aflame, and the pirates and Captain Ishmael were in a deadlock. For Captain Ishmael, there was nowhere to hide. For the pirates, another step forward would mean the loss of a piece of X.

The flames danced higher. Still no one dared move.

Captain Split growled in frustration.

Captain Ishmael dangled the piece of X further over the edge of the ship.

"Another step forward, Split, and it won't just be bait that's been lost forever down this fishing hole!"

Stalemate!

Both captains' eyes locked together.

Watching . . .

Waiting . . .

Hoping to see a crack in the other's resolve.

Unusually it was **McMasters** the mole, left as lookout aboard the **Feroshus Maggot**, who noticed the crack first.

But it was a crack of a different sort—a small crack in the ice surrounding the **PEAPOD**.

One of the massive floes had begun to splinter. There was a **fwhump**, as though from some tremendous impact on the ice from below. The crack grew wider.

Then there was another **fwhump!**

The crack spread all the way up to the **PEAPOD**, and the huge plate of ice released its grip on the ship's hull. She rolled to one side, dangerously close to capsizing and throwing the pirates sideways across the deck. Captain Split braced his bone leg against the gunwale to hold himself steady, and only the long arms of Mr. Clunes kept Milton from rolling overboard.

Everyone on board the **PEAPOD** was now watching the ice.

GwHUMP!

The crack grew.

MwHUMP!

The crack grew some more.

PHHHwHUMP!

Then, with a final ear-splitting crash, an enormous hole appeared and the huge bulk of a great white whale came to the surface.

Captain Ishmael gasped in surprise:

"THE WHITE WHALE!"

Pelf lit his pipe from a burning barrel of tar. "More light green than white, I'd say."

Milton Melton-Mowbray tucked his cutlass back into his breeches and went to look. "I say! You're right, Mr. Pelf—I'd describe it as peppermint colored, myself."

Old Sawbones joined them at the rail.

"Well, I'll be! I'd say this whale was feeling poorly! He seems to have a case of seasickness. Quite rare in a creature that *lives* in the sea as it does."

And, as if to answer them, the whale lifted his head from the water and . . .

BUUUUURp!

. . . let out the loudest belch ever heard.

AND WHAT'S THIS?!

Flying from the whale's mouth?

It's a boat!

A boat pulled by a parachute made from a large luminescent jellyfish. A jellyfish filled with the wind of the loudest belch ever heard!

And clinging to the boat:

"MABEL JONES!" the pirates cheered.

With another lost soul . . .

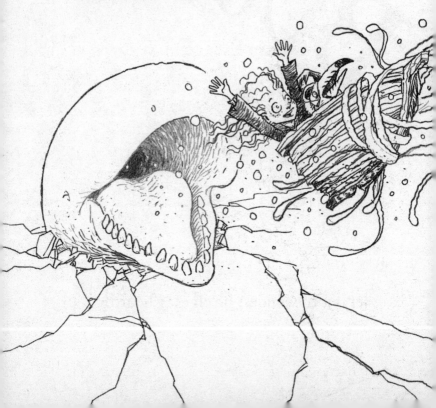

"ABEL, DEAR ABEL!" Ishmael called, tears of joy running down his beak.

"ISHMAEL, SWEET ISHMAEL!" cried Abel. "I have brought you this, saved for four long years."

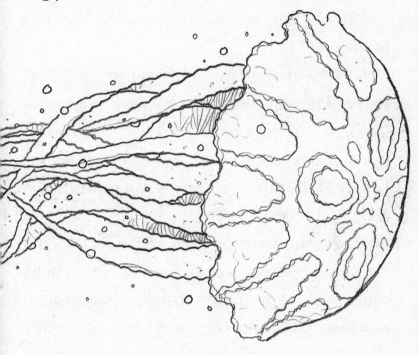

Standing sodden in the remains of the rowing boat so skillfully converted by Mabel Jones, he held aloft the small slice of cheesecake that had caused so much strife between them.

It was still uneaten!

"Please, have a bit," he implored his elder brother.

Clever, resourceful, crafty-fingered Mabel Jones! The only girl ever to have emptied a hundred barrels of fizzy lemonade directly into the stomach of a giant white whale, causing the **loudest belch** ever heard on any of the seven seas.

Praise the heavens—the wind was expelled through the whale's mouth! I would hate to think what would've happened if the wind had been expelled through its bottom. I suppose the pair would have come to a sticky end (so to speak).

As well as freeing Mabel Jones and Abel H. Toucan from the depths of its stomach, the blast from the whale's belch had also broken the **PEAPOD** completely free from the ice *and* extinguished the fire.

Captain Ishmael turned to Mabel.

"I am indebted to you, snuglet. For you have reunited me with my greatest treasure—my brother. If there's anything we can ever do for you, Mabel Jones . . ."

Mabel smiled.

"Actually, there is . . ."

And she held her hand out for Captain Ishmael's piece of X.

Captain Split clomped across the deck. "Hand over the X, Toucan, or I'll split you from beak to tail feathers."

Ishmael looked at him.

"I will give Mabel Jones my piece of X if you first swear a pirate oath on your father's rotten memory that you will leave my ship peacefully."

Split spat on the deck.

"On my father's festering grave, I swear."

Ishmael pressed the piece of X into Mabel's hand and whispered:

"Here it is, Mabel Jones. I give this to you in gratitude for saving my brother."

And with that the pirates returned to their ship. Captain Split was disappointed at the lack of killing but glad at least to have recovered another piece of the X.

As the **Feroshus Maggot** sailed into the distance, Mabel heard angry voices drifting from the **PEAPOD** across the sea.

"I said you could have just a bit!"

"A slice *is* a bit!"

"I meant a bit of a slice!"

Mabel Jones sighed as the **PEAPOD** disappeared from view. All about her were the friendly faces of the pirates, eager to hear the story of her miraculous escape from the belly of the whale.

One, however, was missing. The silent

doorknob-handed villain who had pushed her overboard in the first place.

Now that she was safely back on the ship, Mabel realized that she wasn't angry with Omynus Hussh. If anything, she felt a bit sorry for him. She had, after all, been responsible for him losing his precious hand.

If only I could talk to him and apologize, maybe we could be friends.

But Omynus Hussh was no longer aboard the **Feroshus Maggot**. He was on a secret mission in pursuit of the fourth piece of X . . .

CHAPTER II
The Bestest Thief Ever

*W*hat a view!

The hot sun beats down upon the *Calm Blue Sea*, making it sparkle and shine like a sapphire. A giant castle rises from the gently lapping waters. A castle carved from solid rock, its impregnable walls hiding a civilized world of whitewashed walls and courtyards filled to bursting with vines and olive trees.

See that tall tower?

Peek through that small arched window.

NOT THAT ONE!

I'm sorry, madam. You can return to your bath.

How embarrassing!

I meant *that* window.

Aha! You've found me!

Quick! Here are some underpants: put them over your head and look through the leg holes.

I know, disgusting isn't it? Those underpants have hardly been worn. Who puts underpants in the wash after only one wearing?!

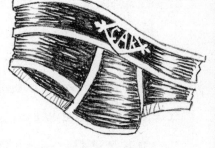

No one would ever know that we are here, hidden safely in a pile of dirty laundry, just in time to see—

Shhh!

The door to the count's private chamber is silently opening!

A shadow enters: the stooping and silent form of Omynus Hussh, the bagger from the **Feroshus Maggot**. We know him well: a treacherous creature—attempted murderer of young Mabel Jones.

See how he creeps around the edge of the room. See how he slides beneath the bed, leaving the dust in place. The only clue to his presence? A tiny scrap of silence where once there was a creaking floorboard.

He's done his homework too, for he seems to know exactly where he is going. A quick glance around the room reveals no threat and he begins to climb the bookcase.

FOOTSTEPS!

In the corridor outside!

Quick and quiet, he curls into a ball and disappears among the shadows. Can you see him? Just there! Between **The Bible** and THE BIG

BOOK OF TORTURE EQUIPMENT.

Always alert. Always watching for danger. His saucery eyes shining with excitement.

The footsteps pass along the corridor, and Omynus Hussh uncurls. His eyes scan the shelf and are drawn to a big red book with a golden clasp.

He looks around and smiles proudly.

"I's the bestest thiever, filcher, pincher, nicker, or stealer that ever's there been on any of the seven seas ever, ever, ever!"

Carefully taking the book down, he opens the cover.

It is no ordinary book, for its insides are hollowed. It is the secret hiding-place of the object that Captain Idryss Ebenezer Split so wildly desires: the second-to-last fragment of the X stolen from his father so many years ago.

Except . . .

THE BOOK IS EMPTY!

"Where is its?"

A tear of disappointment runs down Omynus Hussh's furry cheek. He peers around to check that no one is looking, pulls out a handkerchief, wipes his eyes and blows his nose.

AND THE DOOR OPENS!

A figure appears. **A hooman!**

A hooman like Mabel.

But this hooman is not a snuglet. This hooman is a Fully Grown-Upman, flanked on either side by heavily armed monkeys, their tails flicking in excitement, their sharp pikes pointed at Omynus Hussh.

And what a hooman! So handsome. A complete *dreamboat*. His eyes shine and twinkle like the morning sunlight on a dewy pool. His artfully plucked eyebrows are angled in a way that is both quizzical and confident, like two caterpillars raising their heads to kiss just above the top of his nose. His jaw looks as if it has been carved from a rock that was already quite handsome even before it was dug from the quarry.

The hooman's top lip curls back from his perfect white teeth in disgust.

"Caught in the act! So you're the **foul thief** that has been drifting silently through my castle like a fart from a sickly princess! You were good, loris, but not good enough!"

He pulls a tiny golden comb from the inside pocket of his white jacket and runs it through his perfect hair. Replacing the comb, he lifts a pendant from beneath his shirt.

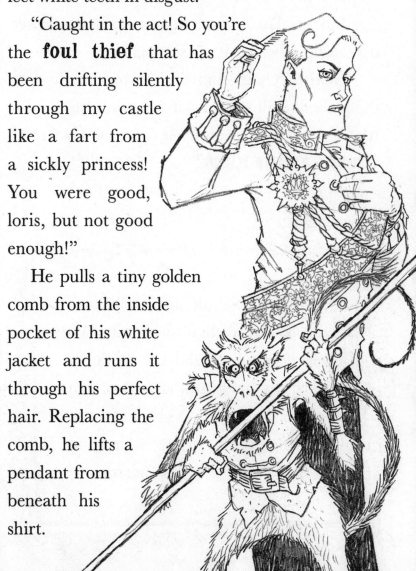

A PIECE OF THE X!

"You were looking for this?"

Omynus Hussh nods glumly. He has never been caught before. It doesn't feel nice.

"Guards, chain him and throw him in the dungeon. We all know what fate awaits those who try to steal precious antiques from the **Castle of Count Anselmo Klack**."

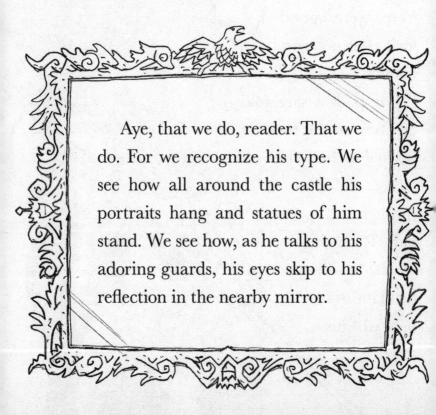

Aye, that we do, reader. That we do. For we recognize his type. We see how all around the castle his portraits hang and statues of him stand. We see how, as he talks to his adoring guards, his eyes skip to his reflection in the nearby mirror.

A vain man. We could have guessed.

Because if there's one piece of advice you take from Mabel's adventure . . .

If you skip every other page . . .

If there's just a single lesson to be learned, it is this:

Never trust a man who washes his underpants after just one use.

So we can very easily guess what fate awaits those who try to steal precious antiques from the **Castle of Count Anselmo Klack**.

A FATE *WORSE*
THAN A FATE
WORSE THAN
DEATH!!

CHAPTER 12
A Friend in Need

*O*mynus Hussh scratched another mark in the
wall of his tiny cell.

He stared longingly at the tiny window, far out
of reach for even the most tricksome of climbing
creatures. Through that window he had watched
day turn to night five times now. Each morning,
a small hatch opened in the door to his cell and a
single piece of dry bread was pushed through.

He picked a maggot from today's bread and
popped it into his mouth. Cuddling his dried
hand, he began to sob.

He sobbed for Captain Split and his crew-mates.

Likes a family to me, they was . . .

He sobbed for the memory of Mabel Jones who, let's remember, was, to his mind, drowned.

It was just a little push. A tiny little push.

And he sobbed for a time long ago. A time he could scarcely remember. A nest among the lush green leaves of a faraway forest. His tiny body curled around his siblings, eight of them, all waiting for their mother's return.

Then bad memories: a wolf's paw, reaching into the nest. The mewing of his siblings as he was carried away into the night . . .

Suddenly his memories were broken by the sound of a key in the door. He sat up, rubbing the tears from his eyes as a hooded monkey entered and the door was closed.

Omynus Hussh squinted through the gloom. There was something funny about the monkey.

Something familiar.

The monkey looked back at the door to check it was closed, then removed its hood.

GASP!

The monkey was actually skilled monkey look-alike Mabel Jones!

Omynus Hussh threw himself to the ground with a scream.

"A ghost has come to finish me off. Back from the dead to claim her rightful revenge!"

He looked up pleadingly from the prison floor.

"Finish me off, Mabeljones, for I was borned

evil, like the captain says, and I deserves what I gets. Just knows this: I's sorry for pushing you off the ship that day. Sorry to the very marrow of my bones that ache with regret."

He pulled open his shirt to reveal his chest.

"Stabs me through the heart, Mabel. Stabs me through my miserable, broken heart."

Mabel smiled kindly.

"It's OK, Omynus. And I'm sorry too. I'm sorry I bit you and I'm sorry you lost your hand. It must be very difficult. It was such a handsome hand."

Omynus Hussh sniffed. "It was, wasn't it?"

Mabel sat cross-legged on the floor.

"Anyway, I'm not a ghost, and I'm here to help you. Not *kill* you."

"*Help* me?"

She took a package from her bag and spoke quickly.

"There is not much time. Take this and . . ."

Mabel leaned forward and whispered some ultra-secret instructions into Omynus Hussh's ear. Then, before he could reply, she stood up. And, as quickly as she had appeared, she was gone.

Then her head poked back around the door.

"Friends?"

"Friends."

Omynus Hussh blinked.

She's alive.

He blinked again.

She came to help me.

He looked at the floor in shame.

After all the nasty I've done.

Then a funny feeling deep inside his chest spread up his throat, like a backward swallow, making his mouth smile in a way that felt nice, rather than all sneery and plotting like usual.

She wants to be my friend!

He hugged Mabel's mysterious bundle tight

to his chest as though it was the most precious thing ever.

No one has ever liked me before.

CHAPTER 13
A Fate Worse Than a Fate Worse Than Death

In the courtyard of the **Castle of Count Anselmo Klack**, a crowd of monkeys had gathered. They grouped beneath parasols, lounging in the sun, all chattering excitedly.

All waiting.

Among them sat Mabel Jones, still undetected in her monkey disguise.

In the middle of the courtyard, a raised platform had been constructed. On the platform sat a wooden block and next to the block stood a brutish-looking gibbon with an executioner's hood and a VERY large ax.

Mabel nodded politely to the heavily bandaged driver of a horse-drawn covered wagon. She stepped to one side as it rumbled slowly through the crowd. The words **Pox-Ridden Tony's Eksecution Popcorn** were crudely written on the side.

The driver took a puff on his pipe, exhaled a toxic green smog and nodded back.

Everyone looked up at the balcony of the count's private chamber.

Watching.

Waiting for the count to appear.

Finally he arrived, the medals on his white uniform glinting in the morning sun. He smiled and his eyes twinkled at the gathered crowd, who sighed in unison.

So much charisma!

The count checked his watch. It was time. He artfully wafted a silk handkerchief in the air and the crowd started to cheer.

Mabel heard the sounds of struggling.

"Please, please takes my head off—just leaves me with my lovely hand!"

Omynus Hussh!

"Not my lovely, lonely little handy!"

He was held tightly by the guards as they pulled him toward the platform.

"It's the only one I gots!"

The guards tied his wrist to the block. Even then the struggling loris tried to shield his precious hand with his neck.

"Anything but my hand!"

The doorknob at the end of his other arm swung uselessly at the monkey soldiers.

The ax was raised.

THE CROWD g a s p e d.

The ax came down.

Omynus screamed.

The crowd winced.

There was the sound of metal slicing through bone and a severed hand spun across the court-yard over the crowd, and landed at Mabel's feet.

She picked it up and put it in her pocket.

Then, just when everyone was applauding the successful cutting-off of the thieving loris's last remaining hand . . .

There was a very loud BANG!

The **Feroshus Maggot**, anchored just off shore, had fired its cannon!

At this signal the driver of **Pox-Ridden Tony's Eksecution Popcorn** wagon whipped off his bandages to reveal the battle-ready face of a savage pirate goat.

Pelf!

From the back of the wagon jumped the other pirates, cutlasses ready and pistols loaded.

At this point a savage battle ensued between the monkey guards and the pirates. I'm afraid this is no stuff for a little 'un. Too much blood and gore can stunt your growth, so let's skip to the end of the fight.

What's that?

You want to hear the **details**?

You think you have the nerve to witness it? In all its grisly and gruesome glory?

Well, all right then. Just for a little bit . . .

See Mr. Clunes, the orangutan! Surrounded by monkey soldiers, each one armed to the teeth. No cutlass for Mr. Clunes, just fists like hams. A swinging blow connects with the jaw of one of the monkey guards and sends him flying. Then another! And another!

He's swatting them away like flies!

See Milton Melton-Mowbray! Who would have thought such a well-spoken and kindly swine could handle a sword with such deadly grace and style. Those fencing lessons at St. Hamlet's School for Rare-Breed Pigs have not gone to waste. Another monkey is pinned to the wall with a thrust of his épée.

"Have at thee, sir!" cries the nicely mannered porker.

To Pelf now. No fancy training for him. Just the school of hard knocks and a degree without honors from the university of life. Pipe still in his mouth, he delivers his blows with cutlass, hoof, and horn. Not the finer stuff like Milton Melton-Mowbray, nor raw brute strength like Mr. Clunes. Just good old-fashioned brawling, honed to perfection by a lifetime of piracy. There's nothing wrong with a **HEAD-BUTT**! Especially when you have horns!

Finally, what creature is this?

It's a snarling ball of **fur and teeth**.

It's a furious **whirlwind of claws and drool**.

It's the most **ferocious** of all the pirates—
C A P T A I N   I D R Y S S   E B E N E Z E R
S P L I T ! On all fours, he leaps from monkey to monkey, his claws scratching and tearing. In the tight and crowded mêlée, he is invincible, and all his foes will feel his rage.

From high above, the count watches the fight with interest as the pirates free their stricken comrade, the no-handed loris. Then he sighs and signals to a monkey positioned safely on the castle walls, well above the scrum.

A warning shot is fired. A bullet ricochets around the inside of the castle courtyard, eventually knocking the pipe from Pelf's mouth.

The pirates look up. All around, high above on the castle walls, the muzzles of a hundred monkey rifles are pointed at them. They slowly stop fighting as the inevitable dawns. They are trapped.

Trapped like rats!

Trapped like rats in a trap designed to be especially dangerous for rats.

The count combs his hair as he watches from the balcony. Smiling smugly, he turns to the monkey guard positioned next to him.

"It pays to be ready for all eventualities, you see."

Then he notices the monkey is pointing a pistol at his belly.

"Yes, I think one should always expect the unexpected," replies Mabel Jones, pulling off her monkey disguise in triumph.

Aye, that's right. It's the cunning, ruthless Mabel Jones!

"Call off the guards or I'll put a ball of lead through yer gizzards!" she commands in pure pirate.

CHAPTER 14
Princess Mabel Jones

The monkeys waited for the order to shoot.

No order came.

Slowly, the pirates began to edge toward the castle gateway. The monkey guards, still waiting for the official order, had to let them pass.

Up in his private chambers, the count twinkled his eyes thoughtfully. He ran his fingers over his chiseled jaw. Finally he scratched his perfectly formed head.

"You're a little girl."

"Yes, I'm Mabel Jones."

"Not a monkey?"

"Definitely not," replied Mabel a little crossly.

"So there *are* other people here!" said the count to himself.

He looked at Mabel more closely and smiled warmly.

"How did you get here?"

"Get where? This room?"

"No. This world! This place! This lawless zoo overrun with foul beasts and beastly fowl."

Mabel Jones smiled proudly. "I was kidnapped by pirates."

The count smiled, his eyes twinkling again. "They're taking anybody these days . . ."

He chuckled to himself.

"And you're looking for my part of the X, yes?"

Mabel nodded.

"We have three bits already, but I need all five to get home."

The count raised a perfectly shaped eyebrow.

"Get home?"

"Back to the hooman world. Once we have all the pieces we can open a porthole and—"

Mabel stopped suddenly. She had said too much.

The count's expression had changed slightly. It was the twinkle in his eye—it had gone.

"And you have found all the pieces but one? How interesting. What a resourceful little girl you must be." The count gazed into the distance as if recalling a memory from long ago. "How I'd love to go back. How people must miss me! You know, I was quite something back then . . ."

The count smiled sadly and removed a chain from around his neck. On the end was a piece of the letter X.

He held it out to Mabel Jones. She went to take it, but he pulled it out of her reach.

"You know, you could live here with me if you wanted."

He looked at her with his lovely blue eyes.

Mabel imagined eating cornflakes with the count and his lovely blue eyes at breakfast. It might not be too bad. They'd probably eat soft-boiled eggs, which were much better than ship's biscuits. Fewer weevils too.

The count smiled again and his eyes twinkled warmly. "Would you like to live in a castle, Mabel?"

She wouldn't have to scrub the deck like she did aboard the **Feroshus Maggot**.

"Would you like to be a princess?"

Princess Mabel!

It had a certain ring to it!

The count's eyes crinkled warmly around the edges. "It must get lonely here. Without your family, I mean."

Mabel nodded sadly. "I miss them."

"Of course you do." The count put his muscular-but-not-too-muscular arm around her shoulders and hugged her a bit. He smelled all clean and soapy. "Maybe I could be your new family?"

But I've already got a family, thought Mabel Jones. And I've already been away for ages, and they'll be so worried.

She looked at the count and his lovely blue eyes . . .

And it was as though they cracked before her gaze and she could see deep within his soul.

She saw the man who had ordered the removal of Omynus Hussh's last remaining hand.

She saw the man who wanted her to stay with him forever in his castle. As a princess?

A prisoner, more like!

Spinning away from his arm, she snarled:

"My name is Mabel Jones. I am a pirate, NOT a princess. And you are definitely not my family! **GIVE ME THE PIECE OF X!**"

Her finger tightened on the trigger of her pistol.

The count smiled politely and bowed a little.
He wrapped the shard of X in his handkerchief
and held it out toward her.

"As you wish, Mabel Jones."

Mabel snatched the parcel and fled.

CHAPTER 15
A Helping Hand

*A*s Mabel fled, she had a strange feeling.

It started as the same type of nagging worry you get if you leave for school having forgotten your PE clothes on a PE day.

As she sprinted through the courtyard, it grew to the size of the nagging worry a parachutist might get after jumping from an airplane, unaware he'd forgotten his parachute.

A monkey guard opened the gates for her.

"What an ugly monkey!" he commented to his fellow guard as they both saluted.

By the time she had reached the eager pirates waiting in a rowing boat, the worry had grown so large she could hardly contain it.

Finally it bubbled all the way out of her mouth. **"The piece of X!"**

It had been too easy! The count had just let her have it. She turned to look back at the castle.

The count was watching her escape from the balcony of the tower. Was he *waving*?

Captain Split looked at her. His evil eye glinted.

"Well? Did you get it?"

Mabel unwrapped the parcel the count had given her.

"Mabel always delivers the goods," declared Pelf proudly.

But Mabel saw differently.

She looked up at the expectant pirates, angry tears of disappointment welling up inside her.

"It's a pebble! A stupid pebble! He must have swapped it."

Split growled a terrible growl.

"Swapped it? You've stolen it for yourself, you miserable little thief!"

"I haven't!" protested Mabel Jones. "The count tricked me!"

"I don't care about the count," snarled Split, stalking toward her, a murderous leer stretched across his face. "I only care about that piece of the X!"

The crew cowered in the rowing boat as Split drew his cutlass.

Suddenly a whispery voice spoke from the other end of the boat.

"Looksy what I've gotted!"

OMYNUS HUSSH!

The cunning creature had snuck back to the boat unseen and unheard. And he was holding the count's piece of X in his hand!

**HIS HAND?!
ONE OF HIS
HANDS IS
BACK ON
THE END OF
HIS ARM?!**

Mabel sighed with relief as Split lowered his cutlass.

"I'll let you off this time, snuglet . . ."

He snatched the piece of X and held it up to the light admiringly.

Omynus Hussh nestled his head on Mabel's shoulder.

"We stealed it together," he said proudly. "Me and Mabel."

Then, so quietly that no one, not even Mabel, could hear, he corrected himself:

"Me and my *friend*, Mabel."

CHAPTER 16
Really, the Bestest Thief Ever

Minutes earlier the count had watched Mabel run from the castle. He smiled to himself.

I'm such a clever man! A silly little girl is no match for me. Even if she is armed and dangerous!

He put his hand in his trouser pocket and pulled out the piece of X. All it had taken to fool Mabel Jones had been a simple conjuring trick he'd learned as a boy.

He placed the piece back in his pocket. He'd have to find a safer place for it now.

All was quiet.

Suspiciously quiet.

The count gazed out over the Calm Blue Sea. Tomorrow he would sail after the pirates on his golden galleon and blow their scruffy boat to bits with his **ornately monogrammed cannonballs**. Then he would take the three pieces of X that Mabel Jones had so helpfully collected, and return home to his own world.

He had no idea that, at that very second, the hand of Omynus Hussh—still very much attached to the arm of Omynus Hussh—was sneaking up inside his left trouser leg and unpicking the stitching of his pocket.

And then, a few moments later, the silentest of lorises was climbing from the balcony to hurry back to the **Feroshus Maggot**.

"But the hand!" I hear you whine. "It was

chopped off! By what witchcraft can a loris grow a new hand?"

And, by chance, Mabel is explaining the trick to her crewmates right now. Let's join them.

"The bundle I gave Omynus was simply a long-sleeved sweater," explained Mabel Jones.

She smiled at Mr. Clunes. "Thanks for lending it to me, by the way. I'm afraid it's a little damaged."

Omynus Hussh continued:

"Then Mabel says to the guard, all softy yes-sir-no-sir, 'It's only fair to let him have his favorite sweater on. After all, you only gets your last remaining hand cuts off once in a lifetime.'"

Mabel blushed.

"All Omynus needed to do was take his dried hand and hold it in his good hand. Then put on the jumper. The long sleeve covered his good hand, with the dried hand sticking out from the cuff."

Mabel drew a quick diagram for the pirates.
"To the casual observer it simply appeared that
one arm was slightly longer than the other."

Milton clapped his trotters together in delight.
"So when the executioner's ax fell to slice off his
hand, it cut through the one he'd already lost! I
say, what a lark."

Mabel smiled proudly. "Then, using the pirate surprise-attack as a diversion, Omynus climbed up the tower to the count's balcony, where he was perfectly placed to steal the piece of X, if need be."

Mabel reached into her pajamas and pulled out the twice-severed hand she had collected after it had been cut off.

"Here, Omynus. I thought you might want it back."

The silent loris shuffled his feet and looked shyly up at Mabel.

"Thank you," he whispered.

Later that day, back on the **Feroshus Maggot**, Omynus Hussh kissed the severed hand good-bye and dropped it gently overboard.

No one saw him do it and no one heard him whisper:

"Bye-byes, hand. I don't needs you anymore. I've got something better now . . . *A friend.*"

CHAPTER 17
The Captain's Leg

Once more, the **Feroshus Maggot** set sail. With four of the five pieces of X in his paws, you'd think Captain Split would've been in good humor.

But no!

With every minute that passed, he grew angrier. And Mabel grew nervous too. The comet was now even farther along its path across the sky, and the X was still incomplete.

Eventually the captain retired to his cabin. The crew could hear him, still shouting, as they toiled at their stations.

Mabel Jones was busy swabbing the deck. A pirate ship must be kept clean and tidy at all times, lest an unfortunate shipmate should tread on a discarded halibut head and slip overboard.

As she was scrubbing around the base of an old barrel, though, something strange caught her eye. Tucked carefully behind the barrel was a small cloth bundle. Peering inside, Mabel discovered a stale old weevil biscuit, two brown apple cores and a hunk of stale bread.

Very strange!

Who could the bundle belong to? Whoever it was must be *very* hungry to be stashing food like that! And somehow she couldn't imagine that any of the pirates liked apples.

Then she noticed something else. Next to the bundle, half hidden by the barrel, was a footprint.

Another hooman footprint . . .

Glancing carefully around the deck, Mabel Jones took her own ration of slightly less stale weevil biscuits from her pocket and wrapped them in the bundle. Then she carefully put the bundle back where she had found it.

And so the **Feroshus Maggot** cut through the waves as if the ship itself were desperate to reach the location of the last remaining piece of X. The piece belonging to the final name on the list:

Old Hoss, from Scrape.

Split re-emerged from his cabin. He could not be satisfied, no matter how many fingers, hooves, or paws were blistered by the burning ropes of a pirate ship at full sail.

"Faster, you lazy whelp!"

His whip lashed out at the bottom of Milton Melton-Mowbray, who was doing his best to climb the rigging (not at all easy with trotters).

"Harder, you sound-less plank!"

The whip lashed the back of Mr. Clunes as he manhandled the anchor into storage.

Even Mabel, who had done so much to help gather the pieces of X, was singled out for harsh treatment.

Actually, she got the worst treatment of all. Every time she crossed Split's path, his single eye would narrow to a suspicious squint. Sometimes he would curse and spit at the deck where she walked.

One time, he'd gone further:

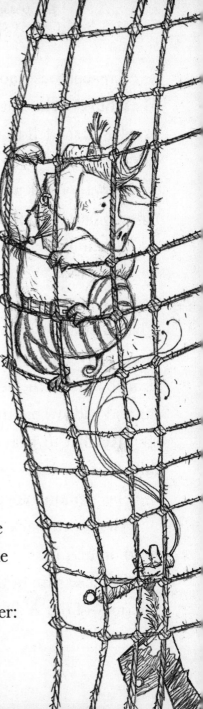

"Treacherous hooman. I got my eye on you!"
His whip **cracked** at her bare feet and he laughed
cruelly as she fell to the deck, nursing her bleed-
ing toes.

Mabel looked up to find his wolf face thrust
close to hers, his foul breath invading her nostrils.

"You and me are going to end badly, snuglet,"
he whispered. "Very badly indeed!"

That night the crewmates gathered on deck to
swap lusty boasts and ghostly tales of the long-
dead beasts of the sea. They spoke of the places
far and wide where they had traveled, and horrors
so **vile** that to hear them would make your tail
fall off (if you had one).

The captain joined their circle.

Pelf leaned back against a barrel. He sucked
hard on his pipe.

"Tell us again of the treasure, Captain. Tell us
the story of the **X**."

"Very well . . ."

The crew huddled closer to the oil lamp, and the captain, fixing them each with a boggle-eyed stare, began his tale.

"One dark and stormy night, more than five years ago, as I was pacing my cabin, a small puffin fell in through the window and collapsed upon my table. My first thought was that it would make a fine accompaniment to my evening meal, for your puffin is a fatsome bird and fries nicely in its own juices. Luckily for the puffin, though, before I could wring its scrawny neck, it managed to squawk my name.

"'Idryss?' it choked. 'Idryss Ebenezer Split?'"

"And then I recognized it! My father's loyal shoulder-bird, **Barrymore**.

"'Barrymore!' I says. 'What brings ye here? What news of my father, the great pirate **GARETH SPLIT**?'"

"'Treachery!' he says, rubbing his throat. 'A mutiny aboard the **Flying Slug**!'"

"The words struck cold into my heart as sure as if I'd been gored by the frozen horn of a tundran yak. For the **Flying Slug** was my father's ship, and mutiny is the foulest of deeds.

"'How did such a wickedness come about?' I asks.

"'It started with the fog,' Barrymore replies. 'We'd been drifting for days, unable to see more than two feet in front of us, when suddenly there was a terrible scraping. We'd struck a rock, though all the charts showed we were leagues from the nearest shore. The hull held true—for the **Flying**

S l u g is a fine, strong ship—but we could not push ourselves clear. And it wasn't long before we discovered that we were not alone . . . A strange creature dwelled alone on that very rock. A hooman!'

"'A hooman!' I cried with a shudder, for the very thought of such creatures disgusts me.

"'Aye, a hooman,' says Barrymore. 'He was stricken with the screaming fevers, bone naked, beardy, and clinging to a metal X. He swore it was the key to a great treasure that he would share with your father, if only he would take him away from that cursed rock.

"'The crew believed that the hooman was a bad omen and we should leave him there to rot, for we already had two hoomans aboard: a cabin boy who'd performed **THE DEED** some weeks before, and a prissy count who'd paid for passage to the Calm Blue Sea. But your father wanted the castaway alive, and he allowed him to join the crew.

"'Five days we waited for wind and tide to lift us free of the rock. But no wind came and the crew grew restless. First they blamed the hooman, then they blamed your father. Finally four of the crew rose up and, in a stroke of the foulest betrayal, **mutinied!**

"'They divided everything on board the ship into five parts, taking one part each and leaving one part for your father—for not even the most villainous of mutineers would leave their captain penniless. Mutinous they may have been, but they were right about the hooman being cursed. The very moment we left the ship, the wind picked up and a wave lifted the `Flying Slug` back into the sea and she sailed away, leaving your father, me and the fevered hooman on that uninhabited rock. Not a bite to eat except the bitter fruit of a single lemon tree . . .'"

Split paused his story and motioned for more rum to be poured into his tumbler.

"That puffin told me a great many more things that my father had learned from the hooman castaway. Secrets of the X that you would never believe. But the one thing he couldn't tell me was the names of the mutineers, for the pirate code forbids snitching. There's no pirate lower than he who tells tales on another like a whiny schoolgirl. But luckily the hooman had written their names down on a piece of paper my father had about his person."

"And that was the list Mabel read for us!" cried Milton excitedly.

The crew looked at Mabel proudly. She blushed and pretended to pick a weevil from the biscuit she was eating.

Old Sawbones jabbed a morsel from his teeth with a rusty chisel. "So the hooman must have written down the names in lemon juice, as that was all he had on the island!"

Split nodded.

"And so my father sent the puffin off to bring

me that list and the piece of the X that the orga-
nizers of the mutiny had left with him. For the
fools had divided the X into five parts too, not
knowing its true powers. And so the parts were
scattered across the seas, until now."

Milton blinked worriedly.

"What happened to your father? Did you not
go back and rescue him?"

"Alas, the puffin couldn't remember where the
rock was. He'd flown further than a puffin ever
should. For all I know, my father and the hooman
are trapped there still . . ." Split grinned and narrowed his eyes. "But more likely the herring gulls
are picking at their bones."

"And the puffin?" asked Mabel.

"Barrymore?" Split smiled a wicked smile. "We
served him that night in a nice red wine sauce!"

He emptied the tumbler of rum down his hairy
throat.

"That's enough stories for tonight, methinks."

While the pirates drifted off to sleep one by one, Mabel watched as the twinkling moonlight shone onto the intricate carvings etched into the captain's bone leg—scenes of battles, mermaids, and sea monsters.

The captain's voice broke the silence.

"You looking at my leg, snuglet? Carved by Old Hoss it was, and sent to me by post after my first peg got woodworm. I guess he felt guilty for mutineering on my father's ship. Or else he was worried I'd come looking for him if I ever found out what he'd done. He's a crafty old sheep. But I'll pay him back soon enough. We'll find him on the island of Scrape tomorrow, and then the final piece of the X will be mine."

"What are those marks?" asked Mabel, pointing to the notches that stretched in a long row almost all the way up one side of the leg.

"These?" The captain traced his claw over them. "These are my tallies. One for each of my kills."

He fixed Mabel with a horrible stare. "I'm running out of space, snuglet. But I'm saving a gap for someone *very* special."

And with that he stood up and **clomped** back to his cabin.

CHAPTER 18
A Sheep Trick

On the island of Scrape, Mabel trudged up a winding path to the ancient church at the top of the hill.

Before she entered, she looked back across the sea. The **Feroshus Maggot** could be seen in the distance. None of the other pirates had come with her on her mission this time. As the rowing boat had been lowered from the ship, Pelf had explained why.

"The folks of Scrape don't welcome us pirates. Those woolly smugglers are a tightly knit bunch.

Best you go alone. With your strange furless face and scrawny arms, they'll never think you're a pirate."

☠

KREEEEEAAAK!

Mabel Jones pushed open the heavy oak door of St. Agnus's Church.

It had taken a while for her to locate the place where she had been told Old Hoss could be found.

A smiling young lamb, crabbing from the cliff tops, had said: "You ain't from around these parts, are you? Old Hoss? His house is in the village of Scrape, just up the chalky path from where I be sat now!"

A laughing sheep delivering the mail had climbed down from his bicycle and said:

"You ain't from around these parts, are you? His favorite tavern was always the **SMUGGLER'S REST**—why not ask in there?"

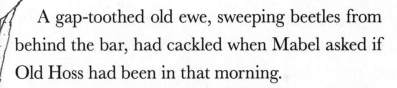

A gap-toothed old ewe, sweeping beetles from behind the bar, had cackled when Mabel asked if Old Hoss had been in that morning.

"You ain't from around these parts, are you? Not a drop of ale has passed his lips for many a month now! You'll find him up at St. Agnus's Church. Tee-hee-hee."

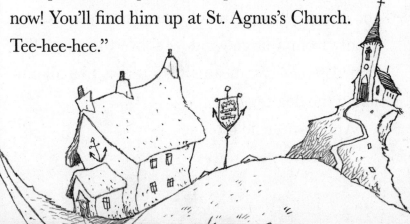

With the ewe's laughter still ringing in her ears, Mabel Jones trudged up the winding path to the ancient church at the top of the hill. She did have some experience with churches, although this time her mission was to recover the last bit of X from a legendary smuggler, rather than to appear as Third Lamb from the Left in her Sunday school nativity play.

And now Mabel stood inside the church. A humble place, lined with empty pews that hadn't felt the warming glow of a devout bottom for many a Sunday. In the corner sat a silent organ, its pipes blocked with spiderwebs and the broken plaster from the collapsing ceiling.

An ancient stained-glass image of St. Agnus the Sheep, patron saint of smugglers, looked down kindly from a large window above the altar. The dulled panes cast beams of sunlight that illuminated the floating dust.

And it was cold too.

Mabel coughed.

There was a scuffling noise and the face of a gray and grizzled sheep-dog appeared over the edge of the pulpit, where he had obviously been sleeping. From his collar, Mabel could see the old dog was a priest.

"Hello?" said the dog. "Have you come for the service?" He looked at a broken pocket watch. "No one's been for such a while now that I'm rather afraid I've not prepared a sermon. I do have some old ones here somewhere . . ."

179

He started shuffling some handwritten notes. "How about 'The Dangers of Sinful Drinking'?"

He shifted a half-empty bottle of holy wine from the pulpit to make more space, cleared his throat, and prepared to speak.

Mabel held a hand up politely to halt the priest.

"Actually, I'm looking for Old Hoss, the smuggler."

The priest peered at her over the top of his cracked glasses.

"Old Hoss, you say?"

Mabel nodded. "The villagers said I could find him here. I need to ask him for something."

The sheepdog pointed at Mabel's feet. "I'm afraid you've been the butt of a rather cruel joke."

"I don't understand."

"You're standing on him!"

Mabel stepped backward and looked at the flagstone beneath her feet. On it was written the legend:

R.I.P.
Old Hoss
Here lies Old Hoss:
Craftiest bleeder that ever lived.
Seldom sheared and never dipped.
Left his debts, but took his
secrets to the crypt.

Mabel stared in shock. Old Hoss was dead, and with him had died the chance of finding the last piece of X!

It had all been for nothing!

Unless . . .

Mabel spoke the words engraved on the tombstone out loud:

"Took his secrets to the crypt."

Maybe there was hope after all!

CHAPTER 19
Going Underground

*H*ave you ever crept through a graveyard in the dead of night with the intention of breaking into an old church?

No?

Have you ever picked the lock of the oak door of the aforementioned church and crept into that damp and dusty house of God, ready to perform the foulest of foul deeds?

No?

Have you ever stepped over the slumbering body of a decrepit canine priest, ready to force open the entrance of the crypt beneath the church?

No?

Well, if that *really* is the case, then I suppose I need to describe the feeling that Mabel Jones felt that fateful night.

It felt like the icy-cold finger of guilt was being drawn slowly down her spine.

It felt like freezing dread had filled her heart and was being pumped around her body until she had no blood—just pure chilled fear flowing through her veins.

But she had to do it. The pirates needed that bit of X.

She needed that bit of X!

It took her a minute of sweaty hard work to pry the flagstone up with a spade she'd found in the graveyard. It made an almighty scraping noise as she pushed it aside to reveal stairs leading down into the darkness.

The priest rolled over, muttered some words from a long-forgotten prayer, then returned to snoring loudly.

Steeling herself, Mabel Jones lit the whale-fat lamp she had brought with her from the **Feroshus Maggot** and began her descent into the depths of the crypt.

She counted twenty steps. And then she counted twenty more.

Still she descended into the gloom.

Eventually the soft glow of her lantern revealed an arched brick chamber. Stacked up against a crack in the wall were four **COFFINS**. The rest of the crypt was filled with barrels and crates.

Each of the coffins carried the name of the poor unfortunate sheep whose body lay within.

REST IN PEACE
BOBBY RAMSDIP

DROWNED IN A BARREL
OF RUM WHILE HIDING
FROM THE RED COATS

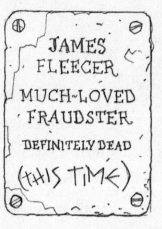

JAMES
FLEECER

MUCH~LOVED
FRAUDSTER

DEFINITELY DEAD

(THIS TIME)

DR. JOSEPH WOOLLEY
CHEESE SMUGGLER

BURIED WITH A STOLEN STILTON

OUR LOSS IS
GREATLY SMELT

Finally, Mabel gingerly brushed the dust from the last coffin.

OLD HOSS

NEVER ONCE

CAUGHT

Mabel's trembling hands reached for the lid. Surely some clue must be contained within.

He took his secrets to the crypt . . .

She paused.

It was no good. She just couldn't do it. Grave-robbing was just too awful a deed. She might be a pirate, but she had to draw the line somewhere.

Suddenly there was a noise above her head. The sound of sheep's hooves on the stone aisle of the church.

Then a voice!

"Old Shepperton's gone and left the crypt open again."

Followed by another voice!

"Wake up, you drunken old fool! There's work to be done."

Then the priest, mumbling apologies . . .

Then—to Mabel's absolute and complete horror—the sound of hooves beginning to descend the stairs.

She was about to be caught red-handed,

grave-robbing! She looked around desperately for a hiding place.

There was only one: the thin space behind the stack of coffins. Blowing out her lantern, she slipped into the gap.

"Did thee 'ear that noise?" said a voice.

"Nope," said another.

"Probably nothing. Thank the Lord, 'cause I don't fancy the slitting of throats tonight. It's too cold. This place gives me the willies, it do."

Now the priest's voice:

"It's a fascinating place, full of secrets! Been used for centuries by us smuggling types."

The second voice cut in angrily.

"You two fools need to blather less and work more. We got to get all these barrels down to the cove by midnight."

From behind the coffins, Mabel heard the shifting of barrels as they were carried up into the church. Back and forth the smugglers came and went until . . .

"This'll be the last one, boss."

"And not before time. The sun'll be up soon. Let's get a move on!"

Finally, the sound of hooves going up the stairs.

If I just wait until they leave, thought Mabel Jones, perhaps I can sneak out after them.

Then a familiar scraping noise and a

CRUNCH

that made Mabel's heart miss a beat and then speed up very rapidly.

The flagstone! Her only exit! She would never be able to move it from below.

"STOP!"

she cried, leaping out from behind the coffins.

"WAIT!"

she begged, running up the stairs.

"PLEASE!"

she sobbed, banging her fists against the sealed entrance of the crypt.

But it was too late. Her small-girl voice was deadened by the thick flagstone that trapped her in this gruesome tomb, and no one heard her.

Putting her back against the large slab, Mabel pushed . . . and pushed . . . and pushed!

She just couldn't shift it. Not a centimeter!

Mabel Jones was trapped! Who knew when the smugglers might come back? It could be hours . . .

Days . . .

Even weeks . . .

MONTHS!

And by then she would be
dead!

Well, at least she wouldn't have to pay for a burial.

CHAPTER 20
Secrets of the Crypt

*A*fter approximately five minutes of frantic panicking, Mabel Jones sat at the bottom of the steps and began to weep.

I'll never get out of here, never mind get home.

Then she dried her eyes.

Then she relit her lantern with a ship's match.

Then she began to explore.

It was obvious to her now that the coffins had all been moved to make room for the smugglers' stash of stolen goods. She felt a *bit* less awful about the idea of opening the coffin of Old Hoss, knowing that he had already been unceremoniously shunted around by a bunch of criminals.

As she continued to look about, Mabel noticed a brick that poked out farther from the wall than the others. The priest's words rang in her ears:

"Full of secrets. Been used for centuries by us smuggling types . . ."

Could it be some kind of mechanism to open a secret smuggling passage?

Mabel got on her hands and knees and pushed the brick.

It didn't move. It was just a brick.

Grabbing hold of a nearby lever set in the wall, she pulled herself up.

A lever!

It moved!

Sure enough, the sound of ancient machinery could be heard.

There was a distant rumbling . . .

Then a nearby grating . . .

Then the sound of running water—like a bath—and a gust of air blew the lantern out.

It was **pitch black**.

The sound of water was getting nearer. Much nearer. And the running bath now sounded more like a gushing torrent.

My name is Mabel Jones and I am not—

Mabel jumped as she felt cold water on her feet. She fumbled with the matches, relighting the lantern on the second attempt. The flickering flame revealed her worst expectations:

THE CRYPT WAS FILLING WITH WATER!

In a matter of moments, it was up to her thighs, and she had to leap to one side as the coffins, buoyed by the rising flood, fell from their stack, splashing into the water where seconds ago she had stood.

The water level continued to rise. Rank and cold, it was creeping slowly up Mabel's body. She tried to wade to the stairs, but it was all she could do to keep her balance as the water rose and rose.

Now it was just under her chin . . .

And still the water rose. All around her, the coffins bobbed like dinghies, threatening to capsize and spill their grim cargo.

It was up to her nose now, and she grabbed at the floating coffin of Old Hoss to keep herself above the water, trying desperately to hold the flickering lantern above her head.

I am going to drown, thought Mabel Jones. **AGAIN!**

Panicking, she shone the lantern around. She gasped as she saw a grotesque and mocking face on the wall before her, but it was only a distorted reflection of her own face in a shiny brass plaque of remembrance.

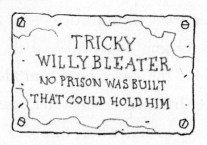

TRICKY
WILLY BLEATER
NO PRISON WAS BUILT
THAT COULD HOLD HIM

Mabel growled with anger.

"I'd like to see him get out of this one!" she snarled, banging the plaque in rage.

IT MOVED!

There was a further creaking of ancient cogs, and a large hole appeared in the far wall. Where before the crypt had been filling with water, now it was filling and draining at the same time, becoming a raging torrent.

Before she knew what was happening, Mabel Jones was caught in the swirling mass of water and coffins rushing from the crypt into the hole and down into a twisting tunnel. She clung on to Old Hoss's coffin, the torrent constantly tugging at her pajamas, trying to pull her under.

Eventually, though, the flow of the river became slower and the coffin's progress more steady. As her eyes grew accustomed to the dark, Mabel could make out brick walls to either side of her.

"It must be an ancient smugglers' tunnel," she said to herself. "A way to get their stolen goods to and from the sea without being noticed!"

At that moment, Mabel heard the distant cawing of gulls. Then she saw a glimmer in the distance.

SUNSHINE!

Light at the end of the tunnel!

But with it came a strange rumbling sound.

Too late, Mabel realized what that meant—a waterfall!

Frantically, she tried to paddle the coffin back up the tunnel, but it was no good—the torrent was too strong! She scrabbled over the coffin. Maybe she could swim against the current! Then, as she tried to get her footing on the lid, there was a terrible sound of splintering rotten wood and . . .

THE LID GAVE WAY

AND MABEL FELL

RIGHT THROUGH!

She had fallen into the coffin!

She could feel dry wool rustling against her skin!

An old leathery tongue drily licking the side of her face.

She was lying on top of the famous smuggling sheep, Old Hoss!

YUCK!

Horrified, she pushed the body away from her in disgust. She had never seen the remains of a dead sheep before, and she was not sure she ever wanted to again.

But what was that?

Old Hoss had a small leather bag around his neck! She snapped it from the length of rotting twine that held it in place.

What was inside? Could it be the missing piece of X?

No! Just a piece of paper!

Forgetting the waterfall, Mabel read the words on the paper.

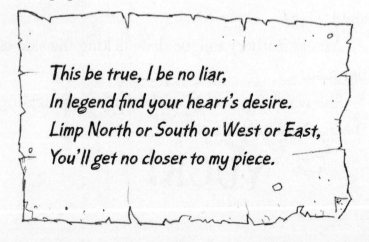

This be true, I be no liar,
In legend find your heart's desire.
Limp North or South or West or East,
You'll get no closer to my piece.

But what did it mean? Could it be a clue to the location of the missing bit of X?

It must be!

Then, before anything else could be done, said, or even thought, Mabel Jones and the coffins were hurled from the darkness of the tunnel—straight out from a hole a very long way up a very high cliff!

Sometimes in an adventure you have little control of what happens next. To my knowledge, there is no way to stop falling down a waterfall once you have begun. There is no cunning pirate trick to save you, no time to remove your pants and fashion a rudimentary parachute, and certainly not enough time to describe the feeling of absolute and complete—

SPLASH!

Before Mabel had even had time to realize she was falling, she was several feet underwater.

When Mabel's swimming instructor had asked her to retrieve a brick from the bottom of the pool while wearing pajamas in order to achieve her bronze swimming badge, she had thought he was crazy.

Why would I ever need to be able to swim underwater in my pajamas?

She didn't think he was crazy now.

As she swam out of the pounding reach of the waterfall, Mabel Jones pledged that, if she ever did manage to get back to her own world, she would buy her swimming instructor a bag of potato chips after her next lesson to say thank you. Or at the very least, let him share some of her pizza-flavored ones.

Old Hoss's coffin floated past and she grabbed it, grateful for a rest.

She had never been so pleased to see a wooden box containing the rotten remains of a dead sheep.

CHAPTER 21
Fishing

The **Feroshus Maggot** was anchored just off the town of Scrape.

The crew were enjoying a day off, confident of Mabel's return from her nighttime tomb-robbing expedition.

Pelf filled his pipe with rancid tobacco and fiddled with his matches.

"She always turns up with the goods, lads."

Milton nodded and cast a fishing line from the side of the ship.

"She's a fine pirate, that gal!"

Pelf puffed out a smoke ring. He watched it float overboard and slowly sink to the sea, where it settled on the exhausted head of Mabel Jones, who was at that moment floating past, draped over a battered coffin.

"Here she is! Told you it would be easy, Mabel!"

Mabel shook her head sadly.

The coffin, with Mabel sitting on it, was winched aboard. At first, the pirates just looked at it nervously. Then Split came out from his cabin and rolled the coffin over with a prod from his bone leg.

The pirates winced as the damaged lid slid off and the body of a long-dead sheep rolled out, its face fixed in a mocking grin.

"Aye, it's him," growled Split. "I'd recognize that crafty leer anywhere!"

He kicked the coffin again.

"Where is it? Where's the piece of X?"

"Erm . . ." said Mabel Jones.

Split fixed her with a boggle-eyed stare.

"You mucked up again, snuglet?"

He stalked toward her, drawing his cutlass.

Mabel backed away until she could back no more.

"I couldn't find the X, but I did find something. I think it's a riddle. A clue to where the last piece is hidden!"

Split snarled.

"What use is a riddle? Words! Puny, tricksy words. It's deeds we need now. Words are for lovesick poets and performing parrots. Words won't stop that comet disappearing from the sky!

"Even a crafty little maggot like you can't wriggle away from this one. This'll be the last time you cost me a piece of the X!"

He pressed the point of his cutlass against her cheek. Mabel closed her eyes tightly. This really was the end of her adventure. Time seemed to stand still.

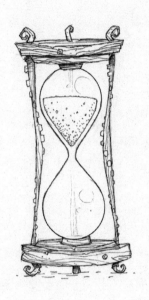

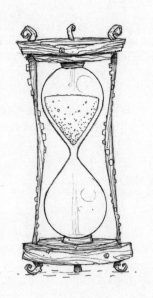

See?

Then a voice spoke.

"Not all is lost, Captain Split!"

Appearing behind them in an impressive puff of smoke stood the tall skull-headed creature that Mabel had encountered all those days ago in the CADAVEROUS LOBSTER TAVERN.

Jarvis the Psychopomp!

The crew gasped.

Captain Split snarled, and the grizzled hair on the back of his neck stood on end.

"And who are you that has the nerve to come aboard my ship without a word of permission?"

Mabel took a now rather damp card from the pocket of her pajamas. Brushing off a piece of Old Hoss, she read aloud:

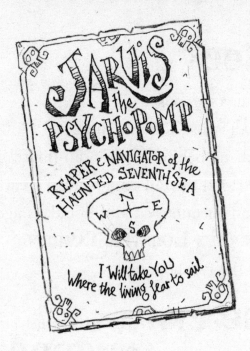

Split looked at Mabel, then up at the Psycho-pomp.

"You know of the **Haunted Seventh Sea**?"

The Psychopomp's skull face swooped down until it was an inch from Split's muzzle.

"I do," it said, its jawbone moving slightly out of time with its words. "And I know why you're going there. You seek the bell tower."

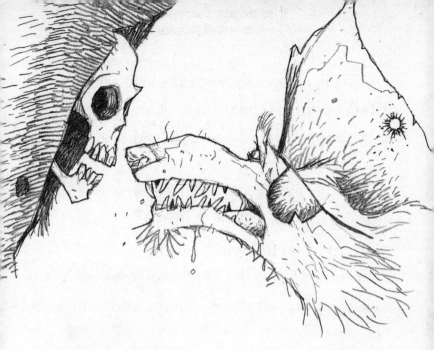

Split's eye narrowed. "And you know where the bell tower can be found?"

"I do."

The captain paused for thought.

"Then I'll trade your life for your help, creature. If you get me to that tower, I won't kill you."

The creature bowed its head solemnly.

"Agreed."

"But what about the missing piece of X?" asked Split, turning back to Mabel Jones.

The Psychopomp reached a long arm into Old Hoss's coffin and pulled out a lump of dull metal, then dropped it upon the deck with a satisfying

CLUNK!

"You mean this one?"

The crew cheered. The last piece of X was found, Mabel was saved, and the adventure could continue.

But something wasn't quite right. Mabel looked at the Psychopomp very carefully. Something wasn't right at all. But she couldn't put her finger on what it was.

A loud splash pulled Mabel from her wondering.

Then another cannonball crashed into the sea nearby. The pirates ran to the rail.

"I say! We're under attack. How unsporting!" cried Milton.

Mabel scanned the horizon.

Five ships.

No, more than five—ten.

No. Even more.

Twenty. Maybe forty!

At the front, an impressive golden galleon hoisted a flag elaborately embroidered with the handsome face of **Count Anselmo Klack**.

"It's the count's armada!" Pelf shouted as he grabbed the wheel. **"All hands on deck!"**

And the ship burst into action.

To the untrained eye, the **Feroshus Maggot** might have seemed a scruffy tub, but she was fast and the crew well drilled. The count's armada, though, was top-of-the-line. The galleons were exquisitely crafted, their sails sewn from the strongest of silks. Agile and fearless monkeys ran up and down the rigging, their dexterous fingers tying and untying knots. Below deck, cannons were being reloaded and aimed.

"Ship ahoy!" shouted McMasters from the crow's nest.

A cannonball fizzed past his nose.

"We're in range of their guns, Cap'n!"

Split growled.

"If we can't outrun them, we'll outsmart them! Hard to port, helmsman! Let's run her through the **Needles**!"

Mabel looked out over the ship's port bow. Just off the shore of Scrape, a wall of stone crept out into the sea. Its jagged edges pierced the water like sharp teeth, making the waves that crashed and frothed about them look like the spittle of a rabid hound. A giant arched rock was the only breach in the wall, and it was straight for this doorway that the **Feroshus Maggot** was headed.

"We have one chance to fit through the arch," cried Pelf. "But, if we can, we be safe, for there is no room for their bloated ships to do likewise."

He blew a smoke ring and watched it dance on the salty breeze.

"The captain's a clever one, that's for sure! The tides are in our favor, for if the count tries to sail around the

Needles' point, he'll be going against the current and then they'll never catch us! NOW STRAP YOURSELF DOWN, SNUGLET! FOR HERE COME THE NEEDLES!"

Mabel ducked just in time to avoid a craggy outcrop on the inside of the arch. There was a horrible scraping of wood on stone, a ripping sound and . . . and . . .

Mr. Clunes leaned out from the ship and pushed against the rock with all his might.

Pelf put all his weight on the wheel. First port. Then starboard.

McMasters ducked into the crow's nest as the tip of the mast bent, then broke against the rocks above . . .

And then they were through!

Mabel looked back. The count's armada was dropping sail and frantically trying to switch direction. One galleon had already come too close to the arch, and the waves had pushed it onto the rocks. The hull had splintered and she was going down.

Milton looked overboard.

"I say, we've lost our name!"

Sure enough, the piece of old board bearing the name **Feroshus Maggot** had been ripped off. It had been *that* tight!

"They'll never catch us now!" crowed Captain Split, as the **Feroshus Maggot** cut through the waves and into the open ocean. "Set course for the **Haunted Seventh Sea**!"

The crew cheered as the Needles slowly disappeared over the horizon. Only Mabel stood pondering. She had found something strange . . .

Beside her on the deck, right where the Psychopomp had appeared, was a light dusting of white powder. And in that powder was another small footprint, just like the ones she had seen before . . .

"What is its?" asked a quiet voice from behind her.

"Hello, Omynus," replied Mabel. "Is this your footprint?"

"No," whispered Omynus Hussh. "It's got nasty little toes, not long and slender like loris toes." He flexed his toes proudly.

Curious, Mabel put her finger in the dust. She smelled it.

Hmmm . . .

Then she licked it.

Mmmm . . .

Powdered sugar!

She threw it into the air and it caught in the breeze like a puff of magic smoke.

Like the magic smoke that had heralded the appearance of Jarvis the Psychopomp.

"Most mysterious," said Mabel.

"Most mysterious," agreed Omynus Hussh.

CHAPTER 22
Rough Passage

*P*oor Mabel Jones.

A single day remains before the comet leaves the sky. The X must be placed in its proper spot before then or she will be stuck in a world that is not her own, destined to remain a pirate and never to see her parents again.

And being a pirate is hard.

If for some reason *you* want to become a pirate, there are some painful truths you will need to learn.

It's not all golden doubloons and swinging from

chandeliers. It's not all drunken shanties and dancing on a dead man's chest. It's not all yo-ho-ho and a barrel of laughs.

Not by a long plank.

Sometimes there are sea voyages that seem to last for years. The wind dies, the sea becomes as still as a clubbed seal, and the hours turn into days.

Then the days turn into weeks.

Just hope that your hold is well stocked and your captain an honest gentleman whom each and every crewmate trusts to lead them safely home to buttered crumpets.

For if not, then ye be lost!

Lost like the crew of the unfortunate **Fero-shus Maggot**, which lists aimlessly on a windless sea, a pale fog cushioning its every creak. The crew thin, hungry, and demoralized. The captain, an already crazed wolf, driven even madder by hunger of a different sort—not for food but for the treasure he seeks.

The sun is about to rise, but for the moment the moon is still queen of the sky, its eerie light dancing across the battered ship.

Only Jarvis the Psychopomp is on deck. Sitting at the bow, where he has sat for the length of the voyage, his eyeless sockets scanning the horizon for signs of the **Haunted Seventh Sea**.

Indeed the **Feroshus Maggot** is a ghost of the ship that sailed from the waters off Scrape. The voyage has beaten and battered her, and her crew sleeps below deck, hunger gnawing at their very souls.

This had been one of those voyages. They'd seen the strangest things.

They'd seen fish with wings skip across the waters.

They'd seen a **kraken**

rise from the depths and grab the last barrel of provisions from the deck, leaving only a faint smell of calamari and an increased rumbling of pirate bellies.

They'd watched as a beautiful mermaid had frolicked in the waves, singing sweet nothings across the foam. Oh, how Pelf's heart had skipped to hear her grunting her song of forbidden love, to see her comb her golden whiskers. And to all this she kept perfect time with the sporadic clapping of her flippers.

At least I think it was a mermaid. It may have been a seal. It had been a long voyage.

They'd seen—

What's this?

A figure rises from below deck. Mabel Jones. She tiptoes up to the Psychopomp.

"Hello, Jarvis. I've brought you this apple to share. You need to eat."

The Psychopomp doesn't move. His eyeholes continue their hollow stare to the horizon. A soft snoring comes from his chest.

Then a moonbeam penetrates the fog. It gleams off a thin length of cotton hanging from the Psychopomp's skull.

Mabel reaches out to gently brush it from his face.

It's attached to his jaw.

She tugs it.

His jaw swings open, as if to speak.

She lets it go.

The jaw clamps shut again.

Then, plucking up courage, Mabel Jones very slowly opens the Psychopomp's robes. Inside, curled around a long stick attached to the bottom of the skull-face, is a boy.

A hooman boy!

A snuglet!

No bigger than her. Smaller, even!

Mabel prods him awake.

His eyes open and he yawns.

"Mom?" he asks sleepily.

Then he sees Mabel Jones and he grabs the robes and stick, bringing his giant puppet back to life.

"WHO DARES DISTURB
THE PSYCHOPOMP?"

Mabel smiles.

"It's no good. I know what's going on, Jarvis."

Jarvis sits back down, his fake skull head hanging limply on the pole.

"I never thanked you for saving me," says Mabel. "You know, with the missing piece of X."

Jarvis sighs. "It's not the real one. I took one of the other pieces from Split's cabin. He'll find out soon enough."

"How long have you been on the ship?"

"I snuck on board just after I met you. I've been hiding in the hold."

"So they were *your* footprints I kept finding," says Mabel thoughtfully.

"Yes," says Jarvis. "Thank you for the biscuits, by the way."

"What do you want with the X?" asks Mabel.

"I want to go home. I miss my mom."

"I do too."

They sat in silence for a bit.

Then Mabel smiled. Jarvis had really fooled everyone. Not bad . . . not bad at all.

Especially for a boy.

"Why are you in disguise, Jarvis?"

"It just helps, that's all. It means I don't get bothered. I've been in this world for a while now, and I've learned that people are more likely to take you seriously if you have a skull for a face."

"How did you get here? Were you taken by pirates too?"

Jarvis nodded. "Five years ago. I was snatched by the bagger of the `Flying Slug`."

Mabel gasped.

"Captain Split's father's ship!"

"Yes."

"Were you there for the mutiny?"

"Yes. I also overheard the castaway's story

because I was secretly tending to him in his fever. That's how I found out that the **X** can open a porthole to the hooman world."

"So that's why you were in the **CADAVEROUS LOBSTER TAVERN**!" said Mabel. "You were looking for Bartok's piece of the **X**."

Jarvis nodded. "But you got it first!"

"Well, you've certainly fooled all the others. Do you *really* know where the **Haunted Seventh Sea** is?"

Jarvis laughed.

"Yes, I used to live there."

"You lived in the **Haunted Seventh Sea**? How come?"

"You'll see when we get there."

At that very instant, a cool wind blew across the ship and, for a moment, the mist cleared and the moonlight lit the waves. Jarvis stood up.

"We're here. Now you'll see what I mean. Look over the side."

Looking overboard, Mabel could see the sea bottom. But it was far from what she'd expected. Instead of a sandy ocean floor, beneath the ship ran roads—real roads, with double yellow lines and cars encrusted with barnacles. She could see the roofs of houses not unlike her own. And, breaking through the waves, tower blocks, church steeples, skyscrapers!

It was as though long ago a great city had flooded, and now lay sleeping beneath the shallow waters of the **Haunted Seventh Sea**.

A cry rose from the crow's nest. "We're here, lads. We're here!"

The crew rolled from their hammocks onto the deck and watched open-mouthed and fearful as the **Feroshus Maggot** drifted through the streets of the long-dead city.

Pelf puffed nervously on his pipe. "I don't like it one bit."

Milton chewed his trotter nervously. "They say this is the realm of the dead!"

Even Mr. Clunes looked out of sorts, although, as always, he said nothing.

Split smiled to himself. It was a particularly wicked smile.

CHAPTER 23
Home

The voyage of the **Feroshus Maggot** was approaching its end.

The pirates believed they had all the parts of the X, but, now she had spoken to Jarvis, Mabel knew differently. She knew Old Hoss's piece was still missing.

The words of his riddle went around and around in her head:

This be true, I be no liar,
In legend find your heart's desire.

Limp North or South or West or East,
You'll get no closer to my piece.

It was the second part that held her attention. She went through it again slowly.

Limp North or South or West or East,
You'll get no closer to my piece.

It seemed as though those lines were aimed deliberately at Captain Split. As if Old Hoss knew that he would come looking for his part of the X. As if he was taunting Split and his limping walk.

Limp North or South or West or East,
You'll get no closer to my piece.

So whichever way he limped, the piece of X would get no nearer.

Mabel was sure she was onto something.

Maybe the final piece of X was not as far away as she had thought . . .

Mabel shuddered. The sunken city filled her with dread, and the fog made her clothes damp and cold. She looked at Jarvis perched at the bow of the **Feroshus Maggot**.

Just like he'd told Split, Jarvis did seem to have a particular knowledge of the streets of the city and confidently shouted commands to Pelf.

"Left at the next crossroads."

"Aye, aye." Pelf pulled hard on the wheel.

"Careful! There's a statue just below the water-line there!"

It was difficult and slow progress, but the crew were skilled. Occasionally the ship would scrape too close to a building, and the pirates would run to that side and push with all their might to fend her clear of danger.

Mabel watched as streets, junctions, and abandoned cars passed under the ship.

"How come you know this place so well?" she asked Jarvis.

Jarvis looked at her grimly. "I said I lived here, remember?"

"Where—in one of these crumbling old towers?"

"No, when it was a *real* city. A working city. The greatest city of them all!"

Mabel looked at the ancient ruins.

"But that must have been **thousands** of years ago."

"You still don't get it, do you?"

Mabel looked confused. Then, as they turned starboard down a wide street, she saw something that chilled her blood.

Something *very* familiar.

Something she'd seen a hundred times before. On postcards, in films, on tea towels, and once with her own eyes on vacation with her parents.

It was Big Ben!

And then she understood.

The pirates took me through a porthole to the future! A future where hoomans no longer exist!

"MOM! DAD!"

cried Mabel Jones.

Jarvis grabbed her by the shoulders.

"It's OK. We can get back. All the way back into the past. We just need the X."

"But we don't have all the bits!" cried Mabel Jones. "We never found Old Hoss's piece. What are we going to do?"

"Don't worry—we'll think of something," replied Jarvis.

And, before Mabel Jones could say anything else, the sound of Split's bone leg on the wooden deck clopped behind them.

Jarvis turned around and raised his skull head in the air as far as it would go.

"BEHOLD! THE BELL TOWER OF THE DEAD AWAITS US!"

CHAPTER 24
Ghostly Forms

The crew stood in silence as the ship gently floated farther into the city. Ancient buildings towered over them on both sides. All around were streets of ruined buildings shrouded in fog.

The **Feroshus Maggot** was following the course of the ancient streets. Once, thousands of shoppers would have navigated the busy pavements. Now, they belonged to the sea. A barnacled bus passed beneath the ship's hull, a school of gray fish darting in and out of its broken windows.

Mabel turned to Jarvis.

"What happened?"

Jarvis shrugged. "I don't know. I've been trying to find out ever since I got here."

Pelf tapped his pipe clean on the rail. "It's as though we drift through the very streets of hell!"

Milton squealed in fright. "Gosh! What's that?"

He pointed a shaking trotter to the top of a building, where a cat sat preening itself.

No ordinary cat. A ghostly cat made from the same mist that shrouded the city.

Pelf chewed his pipe thoughtfully. "That feline looks familiar."

Captain Split trained his telescope on the creature.

"Aye. It's **Maurice**!"

Mabel watched as the cat disappeared into the mist. "Maurice?"

"Maurice was once

the ship's cat on this very vessel," explained Pelf. "He was drowned at sea. In a bag. Nine times. He was a nasty one, that cat. Many an honest pirate had felt his claws . . ."

Milton gulped and wrung his trotters together nervously.

"So it's true that the **souls of the wicked** rest here in this city. Doomed never to move on to the next world."

It certainly seemed to be true. As they drifted toward the bell tower, more and more ghostly faces appeared. At first animals, mostly pirates.

Then hoomans!

Ghoulish bankers looked down from the upper stories of a once-monumental corporate headquarters.

Spectral muggers looked up from the pavements on the seabed.

A line of **dead-eyed businessmen** still stood waiting for a morning coffee that would never be poured.

All watching.

The crew cowered together in a worried huddle on the deck. Only Split stayed firm.

"They can't hurt us now!" He laughed into the mist and shouted, "You've had your chance for wickedness. **It's our turn now!**"

Finally, grappling-lines were thrown from the ship and the **Feroshus Maggot** came to rest against the base of the bell tower.

They

  had

    reached

      their

        destination.

CHAPTER 25
The Bell Tower of the Dead

*M*abel looked up at the sky. The comet was nearly out of sight. Its bright white glow was starting to disappear beyond the far horizon.

Time was running out, but entering the bell tower was not going to be easy. The original entrance was submerged some feet underwater, so a long plank was balanced from the ship to a salt-stained stone windowsill.

They went across it one by one.

Split went first, clutching a bundle with the

pieces of X inside. His bone leg skidded on the plank, but his balance remained true. Smashing the window with his good leg, he climbed into the bell tower and out of sight.

Then Pelf crossed on his stomach. Inch by inch.

Milton **skipped** delicately along the plank on all four trotters.

For McMasters, it was an easy task once he'd been pointed in the right direction.

Old Sawbones took his time, pausing for courage in the middle. The plank **creaked** worryingly.

Mr. Clunes bounded across in leaps. With his last bound, a splintering noise could be heard from the plank.

"Where's Omynus?" asked Mabel.

The loris's face looked down from a window high above. In typical fashion, he'd crossed the plank unseen and unheard. He smiled shyly at Mabel.

"Quickly, quickly, snuglet."

Now just Jarvis and Mabel were left. And the plank had a slight kink in it.

Jarvis looked at Mabel.

"After you. I'll hold this end. It will be safer."

"No. After you! I'll hold it safe!"

They glared at each other.

Jarvis took a coin from his robe. "Let's toss for it."

Pelf's head poked from the window. "You'd better hurry up, mateys. We've got trouble closing fast!"

As he spoke, the mist swirled aside to reveal the impressive hull of a golden galleon drifting silently toward them. And then came the sound of whips and shouting.

"Steady as she goes. Load muskets!"

A figure could be seen on the prow of the golden galleon. There was no mistaking that heroic pose, that hair blowing in the breeze, or that face—timelessly striking, as if carved from the hardwood of the handsome tree.

The count!

He had found a way around the **Needles**, though his armada was diminished for sure. Where before there were forty ships, now just ten sailed into sight between the towering buildings.

"Quick!"

Mabel and Jarvis looked at each other and ran across the plank together.

Halfway!

Almost there!

244

And suddenly they were falling hand in hand toward the sea. The leering faces of the long-since dead looked up from the seabed and prepared to welcome the unfortunate children to their watery graves.

But, just before they hit the water, Mabel felt a large hairy hand around hers and she was jerked upward.

MR. CLUNES!

Mabel held tightly to Jarvis's hand, even though it felt like she was being torn in half.

Then, with an armpit-splitting jerk, Mr. Clunes pulled them both inside the bell tower.

"There's no time for horseplay," snarled Captain Split. "We've got to get to that bell!"

Up the dry and dusty steps they ran.

Up . . .

Up . . .

And up . . .

Finally the stairs opened out into a large chamber illuminated by four huge circular windows—the reverse side of the clockface! Around the room and rusted in place, huge cogs hung—the machinery that once turned the hands of the clockface. A giant bell was suspended in the middle of the room.

Milton clapped his trotters together in excitement, then pointed to one of the windows.

"I say! Look, that clockface is missing an X! This must be the place!"

Split smiled. "And soon the treasure will be *mine*." He looked at Mabel through wicked, smiling eyes. "And then we can go home. Where everything is lovely and safe and snug."

Mabel frowned. Something about the way Split was talking made her feel uneasy.

Pelf looked around the room. "So where does the treasure appear? When do the jewels rain from the sky?"

Old Sawbones grinned. "When can I bathe in a blood-red puddle of rubies?"

Everyone looked at the captain.

"You fools!" growled Split. "The treasure is far more valuable than mere baubles and trinkets. The X is the key to an ancient machine built here in the dim and distant past by the fevered hooman rescued by my father from that rock."

Split motioned to the workings of the bell tower.

"One night, long ago, with the comet in the sky, he rang the bell and opened a porthole that brought him from that ancient time to the present day!"

"It's a time machine!" gasped Mabel.

Split laughed wickedly.

"Yes! A ship to voyage through the misty seas of time. But the foolish hooman had forgotten the comet. Its strange influence interfered with the machine.

The bell opened a porthole through time, sure enough, but"—he bared his fangs in a deranged smile—"it also woke the dead souls that haunted this accursed city!"

Mabel blinked, and blinked again.

"The dead?"

Split laughed.

"The wicked dead! And they were grateful for their alarm call. For whoever wakes them becomes their commander. The general of an **invincible army**—for the dead cannot be killed again.

But the hooman was puny-hearted, as hoomans often are. He was gripped by the frights, scared of what might be done with such power. And so he took the X from his machine and fled with it to the furthest, most remote rock he could find, where he thought it would be safe from the forces of evil . . ."

"And that's where your father found him," said Mabel.

"Exactly. And now the X is mine, and its treasure—an army of ghostly soldiers—will be at my command. And where do you think I plan to lead them, snuglet?"

Mabel gasped.

"Home!"

Split smiled.

"Aye. When the porthole is opened, I will lead them to your world. *Imagine* the possibilities! The hooman world is rich in treasures . . . treasures beyond the imaginations of us simple pirate folk."

Split's one eye boggled at the thought. "When the bell tolls, it will signal the dawn of a new age: the age of Captain Split and his

invincible army of the dead."

Triumphantly, he thrust the clanking bundle of fragments into the air.

"IDRYSS EBENEZER SPLIT: KING OF THE PAST AND THE PRESENT! CROWN PRINCE OF THE FUTURE!"

CHAPTER 26
Raising Hell

*P*oor young nose-picking Mabel Jones. She had never asked to be a pirate. She had never even asked to be a hooman. But here she was. Standing between Captain Split and his wicked plan for world domination.

Split emptied his bundle onto the floor and began to assemble the bits of X.

Mabel looked at Jarvis.

He's still one piece short!

Old Hoss's riddle popped into her brain:

This be true, I be no liar,
In legend find your heart's desire.
Limp North or South or West or East,
You'll get no closer to my piece.

She knew the final piece was close. Wherever Split limped, he got no closer to it. But what was the legend the riddle spoke of?

Split held the **X** aloft. "It is complete!"

Old Sawbones looked puzzled. "I think there's a bit missing, Cap'n!"

Split took the **X** apart and reassembled it.

Milton scratched his head. "It's still not quite right, sir."

Split growled a growl so **hideous** it made the crew shrink to the edges of the room.

"There's one piece missing . . ."

His eyes flicked to each member of the crew. In turn they cowered before his gaze.

Finally he looked at Jarvis.

Then at Mabel.

Then at Jarvis again.

"We've been betrayed, mateys! That last fragment—the Psychopomp's fare! Some trickery occurred, methinks! Some **deep** trickery . . ."

Jarvis's hollow eye sockets met Split's one-eyed glare. He said nothing.

Then Split pounced.

Faster than a smuggler's wink, he was upon Jarvis, ripping savagely with his teeth and clawing with his back paw. He tossed the Psychopomp around until all that was left were scraps of cloth and a shattered skull.

But that was all!

No guts. No blood.

Mabel smiled. Jarvis must have snuck out of the back of his robes while no one was watching. He really was quite clever, for a boy.

Split stepped back from his victim, looking confused.

"There be nothing to that ghoul! Just a head! A most unsatisfactory kill, but still a kill nonetheless. And I've never killed a Psychopomp before!"

He marked a tally on his bone leg—in the very last space he had.

Pelf coughed and spat on the floor. He was looking out from a hole in the clockface.

"There'll be more killing before the hour is out, I'll wager. The count's soldiers are coming in!"

Split snarled.

"I'll not let that perfumed Prince of Priss steal what's rightly mine. By fair means or foul, this bell will be rung!

"One . . .

"Two . . .

"Three . . ."

And he threw himself with all his might upon the huge bell.

CHAPTER 27
The Terrible Klank

KLAAAAAAAANK!

CHAPTER 28
The Consequences of the Terrible Klank

*L*andlubbers will argue that the nicest sound in the world is the birdsong that heralds the first dawn of spring.

A worm would disagree.

Mothers may say the sweetest sound is the laughter of a newborn baby.

Aye, I know. 'Tis hard to warrant, for such a sound cuts through a pirate's stomach and raises bile in the throat. I, for one, find it hard to even walk within earshot of a nursery without pausing to be sick on the pavement.

However, worm, mother, seafarer, or otherwise, you could not fail to agree that the most horrific sound in the world is the terrible **KLANK** emitted by the bell known as Big Ben when it is rung by force rather than the carefully calculated physics of its ancient machinery.

It is a sound that penetrates your skull and rattles your brain. A sound that makes your teeth shrink back into your gums. A sound so awful it is indeed enough to wake the dead.

Split glanced hungrily around.

"The porthole! The porthole! Has it opened?"

He looked outside. A smile crossed his lips.

"The dead are awakening! **My army is assembling!**"

Mabel peered out from a small window in the clockface.

This didn't look like the obedient army of ghosts that Split was expecting.

Where before the ghosts had numbly watched the **Feroshus Maggot** drift up the sunken streets, now the mist swirled and twisted into angry forms.

First, animals in clothes—a band of ghostly pirates and criminals brandishing the weapons they'd held at the moment of their deaths.

Then hoomans. The wicked who had drowned when the city flooded—muggers, thugs, businessmen, and politicians. Then people from earlier days of the city: **medieval knights** on spectral steeds; *Vikings* swinging their mighty axes; ROMAN SOLDIERS with rusting javelins.

All dead.

All wicked.

And all exceedingly angry at having been awoken by the terrible **KLANK**.

Pelf took a puff on his pipe.

"The bell tolled flat! The machine has misfired!" He looked at the captain. "There is no porthole been opened. You've doomed us all, for you have enraged the dead!"

And it was true.

From the windows of broken buildings the ghosts climbed, from the seabed they rose, until the ships of the count's armada were swamped in the angry mist of specters.

The defenses of the warships were of no use against the dead. Cutlasses and musket balls passed through the ghostly forms. And yet those same forms seemed solid enough to the count's monkey soldiers when spectral fingers gripped around their necks, throttling them; their ghostly weapons seemed sharp enough as they were cutting them down.

One by one, the count's ships were overwhelmed. Where before the monkeys were trying to get into the tower to attack the pirates, now they were calling for help.

"Open the door!"
"Save us!"

But it was too late.

Soon only the count's golden galleon remained afloat, an empty ghost ship, doomed to float forever in the **Haunted Seventh Sea**.

Then the souls of the wicked dead turned their eyes upward to those who had dared wake them from their fitful slumber. Slowly they drifted toward the tower . . .

Milton wept quietly into a silken handkerchief.

"Oh, Mother. Shall I never see you again? How I wish I could turn back time. Oh, for one last glimpse of my dear parents and sweet little Hambelina. She did nothing to deserve such a villainous, piratical sibling!"

Pelf sighed. "Aye, I never got to have that farm in the mountains either." He blew out a cloud of mournful smoke.

The other pirates shook their heads. All of them had unfulfilled dreams and hopes. McMasters's bed-and-breakfast. Old Sawbones's nursery for zebra foals. All of them had regrets for their lives of crime.

But Mabel Jones wasn't regretting.

She was too busy with a thought.

One of those little germs of genius that, if nurtured in the grime of logic, can grow into an exploding emission of inspiration!

> *This be true, I be no liar,*
> *In legend find your heart's desire.*

The words written and left in the grave of Old Hoss, that crafty old ram. The only pirate on the captain's list who had defeated them! The only one whose piece of X was still unaccounted for.

But what did the words mean?

The idea-germ started to multiply . . .

Split noticed Mabel thinking to herself and stalked toward her with a snarl.

"She's been a curse on my ship since she stepped on board!"

In legend find your heart's desire.

What legend?

"I'll slit her from nose to navel."

Legend . . .

"I've killed so many my bone leg is full. What's one more life? And a measly little snuglet at that!"

Legend . . .?

"One more murder before the dead claim me for one of their own!"

Leg . . . end . . . LEG END!

"That's it!" cried Mabel Jones. "That's why wherever Split limps, he gets no closer. Because he already has it! The missing piece is in—"

And then Split sprang. A ball of fury, ripping through the air with a horrifying howl.

Mabel spun away and drew the cutlass from her belt. Split's bite missed, but his claws sliced three deep red scratches across her cheek!

He turned to face her again, ready to pounce. Mabel held her cutlass tightly. Her eyes narrowed with determination, even though she knew mere bravery would be useless against Split's rage.

Suddenly Split was whipped away from Mabel.

Mr. Clunes, the silent orangutan, held him suspended by the throat.

"If we die tonight, we die without the blood of a crewmate on our hands."

Mr. Clunes's first words in all the twenty years since his hairdressing salon had burned down and he was forced by poverty into a life of **PIRACY**!

Pelf stepped forward.

"Aye," he said. "We've had enough of your bullying ways, Split. You've done nothing but lead us to our deaths. And on a fool's errand at that."

Split shook himself free from Mr. Clunes's vice-like grip. "A mutiny? A **MUTINY** is it?"

Mr. Clunes folded his huge muscular arms. "Aye. It appears so. A mutiny!"

Split leaped again, this time at Mr. Clunes. This time faster, higher, and even angrier. The two creatures, locked in a deadly embrace, tumbled against the clockface. There came an awful noise of cracking glass and they fell through.

NO!

Plummeting to their deaths?

A ledge!

The other pirates rushed to save their crewmate. For mutiny, once begun, must be seen through to the end.

Split gets the upper hand. He twists from Mr. Clunes's grip and prepares to deliver the killing blow, but pauses for a triumphant smile.

But what's that behind him?

A shadow within the shadows. A scrap of silence amid the din of battle.

OMYNUS HUSSH!

He rushes forward to deliver a push to Split's hindquarters. Just enough to knock the captain off balance, tottering toward the edge. His bone leg catches in a hole and for half a second he hangs at an angle from the top of the tower.

Then there is the sound of splintering bone. Split's intricately carved false leg—fatally weakened by one tally mark too many—fractures, then

SN APS!

A flash of fear crosses Split's crazed eye, boggled from a lifetime at sea.

Then he is falling . . . falling into the mist.

Captain Idryss Ebenezer Split is no more.

Only the bottom half of his bone leg remains, still wedged in the hole that was his undoing.

Mabel reaches down to help Omynus in from the ledge. She reaches out with the cuff of her pajama sleeve and wipes a tear from his furry cheek.

"Thank you, Omynus."

The door to the bell tower bursts open and Jarvis appears.

The crew look confused. "Another snuglet?"

But there is no time to explain.

"We're overrun!" yells Jarvis. "The ghosts are inside the tower!"

He turns and bolts the large door as the crew huddles together in despair, for there is no hope against foes who cannot feel the sharpened edge of a cutlass or the dull, leaden impact of a musket ball.

Wrong!

There is one hope. Mabel Jones! She steps forward and pulls Split's bone leg end from the hole. Holding out her hand, she tips it up and from the hollow center of the bone there falls . . .

THE

LAST

PIECE

OF

THE

X!

"Old Hoss hid it in the one place he knew Split would never look," grins Mabel. "In the bottom of his bone leg! That's what the riddle meant! 'In *leg end* find your heart's desire!' Split's leg end!"

Quickly Mabel assembles the X and passes it to Omynus Hussh. Skillfully, he climbs through the broken glass, up the minutes on the clockface, to the empty space where the missing X belonged.

"It fits! It fits!"

The bolted door creaks under the weight of the ghosts pouring up the steps of the tower.

Slowly the sound of machinery can be heard. A grind of ancient metal on ancient metal. The pendulum in the bowels of the ancient bell tower begins to swing.

Cogs begin to move.

The door is breached and the ghosts pour through, arms outstretched to embrace the unfortunate pirates.

And somewhere, far above, a comet is about to leave the sky.

CHAPTER 29
The Sonorous Bong

BONNNGG!

CHAPTER 30
Repercussions of the Sonorous Bong

A ghostly hand grabbed Mabel Jones's arm. Cold and icy fingers dug into her flesh.

Another hand reached out toward her neck. She closed her eyes.

Surely this time it really is the end . . .

☠

You don't mind if I help myself to a pickled onion, do you? It seems a shame to let them go to waste, and this seems a good place to take a short break from the story.

Ahhh, pickled onions.

Let me tell you about pickled onions! The secret, of course, is in the vinegar. One must choose the—

What?

You don't want to hear about pickled onions?

You want to hear about the imminent death of Mabel Jones?

Oh, very well—where was I?

Ah yes . . .

☠

Another hand reached out toward her neck. She closed her eyes.

Surely this time it really is the end . . .

But it wasn't.

"Mabel?"

"MABEL! Open your eyes." It was Jarvis.

I'm ALIVE!

The ghosts stood before her, motionless.

Pelf looked at Mabel. "The dead are at your command, Cap'n Jones," he whispered.

For the splittest of seconds, Mabel imagined what it would be like to have her own personal army of ghosts.

I could be the queen of the dead.

I could have a crown of bones.

I could be the most powerful girl that ever lived.

Then Jarvis's voice broke her from her daydream.

"Look! The porthole."

A shimmering window had appeared in the corner of the bell chamber.

Mabel laughed happily. "The way home!"

She turned to the ghosts, and in her most queenly voice commanded:

"RETURN TO YOUR WATERY GRAVES, OH WICKED ONES!"

The nearest ghost looked at her through blank eyes. Then, slowly, he and the other ghosts drifted from the bell chamber.

Pelf blew a celebratory smoke ring.

The mist was settling, and the city of the dead was returning to sleep.

"Come on," said Jarvis. "It's time for us to go home."

Mabel Jones turned to the pirates. They might have stolen her from her home, her family, and her whole life, but she had grown to love them. She pulled them into a big hug. All except one.

"Where's Omynus? I must say good-bye to Omynus!"

But there was no sign of the silent loris.

"I don't think he likes good-byes, Mabel," said Milton, drying his eyes.

Jarvis tapped her arm lightly. "We must hurry!" he said, pointing out of the window. "The comet's light is fading!"

The two friends held hands, and prepared to step through the port-hole and into the safety of their own world.

Then a familiarly warm voice spoke from a familiarly handsome face . . .

"I think you've caused enough trouble, Mabel Jones. Step away from the porthole. And that goes for the rest of your mangy flock of vermin!"

It was the count!

He was alive. And he was pointing a pistol straight at the heart of Mabel Jones!

CHAPTER 31
The Count's Revenge

So, dry your eyes, reader. The story hasn't finished yet. In fact, it's taken a sudden turn for the worse. And, typically, a hooman Fully Grown-Upman is behind the twist of fate. A hooman who spent the last half-hour quivering and shaking beneath his luxury silk duvet, hidden from the soulless eyes of the dead.

But now the dead have returned to their eternal sleep. And now the count is angry.

Very angry.

"Did you think you could leave me here, Mabel? With these *animals*?!" He gestured at the crew dismissively. "A man of my standing? I've been stuck here too long. I was somebody once, you know."

His eyes had a faraway look.

"Ah yes, the lights, the cameras, the **PAPARAZZI**. Look closely." The count angled his head to the side. "Recognize me now?"

Mabel looked at Jarvis.

They both shook their heads.

Mabel scratched her nose thoughtfully. "If you want, you could come through the porthole with us."

Jarvis nodded. "We can all go back home! But we must hurry. Before the porthole fades."

The count smiled.

"Together? How sweet."

He leered at the two children.

"But you two are going nowhere! I don't need

any supporting characters in the story of my triumphant return!"

He pointed the gun at Mabel.

It happened so quickly.

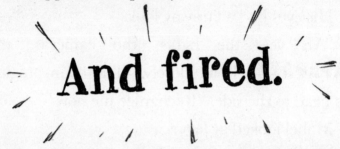

And fired.

In a blurring of silent loris, Omynus Hussh launched himself from the shadows and into the path of the bullet.

Then he collapsed in a heap.

The count swore. "**Blast!** I've shot the stupid squirrel thing by mistake!"

And then the pirates were upon him.

There was a brief struggle, another shot from the pistol, and then the count lay still.

Mabel knelt by the body of Omynus Hussh.

His eyes flickered open . . .

His lips moved and, though they made no sound, Mabel understood.

"I love you too, Omynus." A tear fell from her eye and landed on his furry cheek. "Please, please don't die!"

Jarvis touched her on the shoulder. "The porthole is fading. We must leave now!"

Omynus Hussh blinked slowly, his face twisted in pain.

"Go! Go, my snuglet!" he whispered. Then his eyes closed.

Mabel pressed her head against his chest, but there was no sound.

She looked at the pirates, tears falling from her cheeks. "He's dead!"

Pelf smiled sadly. "But he died a happy loris, Mabel—and dying in battle is the pirate way and it will come to all of us eventually. Even you, maybe! So go! It's been fine knowing you, and you'll be missed, but your place is not in this world. Farewell, Mabel Jones."

And with that Jarvis pulled her into the porthole.

☠

Now Mabel was falling. Falling through the night. Or was she floating **upward**? It was hard to tell in all that fog.

An invisible force pulled her away from Jarvis.

"Where are you going?" she cried.

"Back to my own home," answered Jarvis, waving. "See you around, Mabel Jones!"

And he was gone.

And she was back. Back in her room.

It was night.

She could hear the neighbors' TV.

She could hear the cars driving up and down the busy road. And, when she pressed her ear against the floorboards, she could hear the scuttling of mice.

Mabel Jones crept onto the landing and pushed open the door to her parents' room.

Her mom stirred in her sleep.

"Mabel? Go back to bed, Mabel."

Her dad rolled over, letting out a loud snore.

"What's going on?" he mumbled. "Listen to your mom, Mabel. It's the middle of the night."

"OK," said Mabel, smiling. For she knew no

time had passed since she had been taken—no time at all.

She tiptoed from the room, pausing outside to peek back in.

"I love you, Mom. I love you, Dad."

Mabel Jones was home.

Really home.

EPILOGUE

*A*lthough she looked for Jarvis, Mabel couldn't find him. Not in London. Not in England. Not at all. Maybe she was looking in the wrong way. Maybe she was looking in the wrong time.

But she often looked out from her bedroom window on foggy nights and thought of her crewmates. Had they sailed off into the sunset on the count's golden galleon and given up their lives of piracy? Her only mementoes from the voyage of the **Feroshus Maggot** were the three scars Split had scratched down her face. They looked rather heroic.

And Omynus Hussh? Mabel would never forget him. And memory is a powerful thing, for when something is alive in your memory it is never truly dead. His last heroic deed stayed with her, as clear as the silence she heard when she had listened for his heartbeat that tragic day.

Just silence.

a suspicious silence . . .

ACKNOWLEDGMENTS

 *Special thanks to . . .*

David Lucas, without whom I'd have given up writing long ago. **Paul**, my agent, **Laura**, **Ben**, **Jacqui**, **Joanna**, **Wendy**, and everybody else at Puffin and Viking. **Ross** for his amazing illustrations. **Mandy** for the text design. All the people that read this and the awful stuff that never made it this far, especially **Washy**, **Rat**, big brother **Rich**, and everyone at my writing group. **Graham**, **Martin**, and everyone at Polymath Digital. My **mom** and **dad** for having a bookshelf filled with amazing stories. Last but not least, **Ellen** for refusing to listen to me talk about writing a book until I had actually finished one.

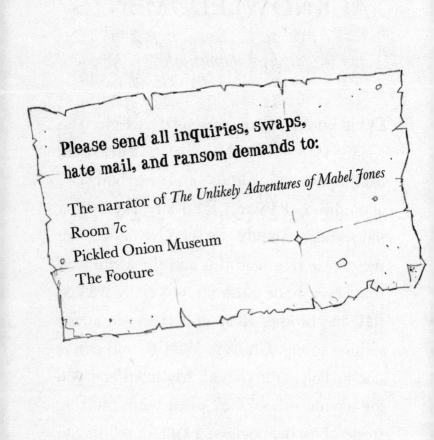

Please send all inquiries, swaps, hate mail, and ransom demands to:

The narrator of *The Unlikely Adventures of Mabel Jones*

Room 7c

Pickled Onion Museum

The Footure

TURN THE PAGE
TO READ AN EXCERPT FROM

MABEL JONES

and the

FORBIDDEN CITY

CHAPTER 1
Fetch Her, My Foul Creepers

$\mathcal{M}$abel Jones scratched her armpit thought-fully and peered at the **extraordinary** creature before her.

It's a funny-looking thing, all wrinkled and fat and helpless. Like a beetle grub. Kind of slimy, but kind of cute too.

Her baby sister, Maggie, snored gently and blew a snot bubble from her left nostril.

Babies can be quite disgusting, thought Mabel, absentmindedly picking her own nose and

wiping her finger on the wall. Especially when you have to share a bedroom with one.

She yawned, climbed into bed, and fell asleep, totally unaware that something quite **dreadful** was about to occur.

Which (of course) is why *we* are here.

Slide open the window and **squeeze** inside.

I think we're just in time. We wouldn't want to miss any dreadfulness.

Creep silently to the wardrobe and **press** your gristly earhole trimmings to the door. Can you hear the distant sound of drumming?

A **frenzied** beat.

It grows **louder** and **louder** still!

What's this? **Chanting too?**

Just when I thought it couldn't get any worse. This must be some kind of witchcraft.

I don't like this. I don't like this one bit.

Far, far away, a long fingernail scrapes along the words of a letter—a letter written during a previous **most unlikely** adventure by the very same Mabel Jones we see safe and snug, asleep in her room. A letter bottled and corked and thrown over the side of a pirate ship into the rolling seas. For months it bobbed on those waves, years maybe, until it washed up on a faraway beach to be found, swapped, sold, stolen, then lost and found again, before it finally reached the hands of this strange and wicked creature.

Cracked and painted lips silently mouth the words of the letter. Then the fingernail pauses as it reaches the end of the final sentence, where an accidental memento has been left.

A single hair—a Mabel hair—is carefully removed from the letter and sniffed.

Fresh snuglet . . .

Fresh enough for dark magic.

The grim smile widens to reveal ancient crumbling teeth. The drumming has stopped. The chanting has died to a soft murmur. And now a voice speaks, in soft yet cracking tones—like honey poured thick on burned toast—whispering an incantation:

"Fetch her, my foul creepers. Bring me the one called Mabel Jones . . ."

So brace yourself—for a wicked seed has been planted and, though its roots are firmly embedded in the future, its shoots and vines are winding through the hot and steaming mists of time into the present.

Quickly! Press your puny weight against those wardrobe doors, child. You must prevent this foulness from occurring.

Alas, it is futile. Your scrawny body is no match for the strength of **dark magic**.

It's time for the secret weapon. Have you brought the powdered beak of a heartbroken swan? Quickly mix it with your vial of hedgehog tears to make a paste, then mark the sacred sign upon—

What?

You don't have either of these things?

Really?

Really, really?

Then all is lost!

A thin white shoot sprouts through the gap between the wardrobe doors. It grows fast and strong, and splinters the wood. A vine has formed.

The vine branches.

Its branches branch.

Then those branches branch some more branches.

And the branches of the branches of the branches branch once more until the room is filled with curling vines that wrap and twist around bookcases and chair legs, pulling all they find closer to the open doors of the wardrobe, like the tentacles of a **starving octopus**.

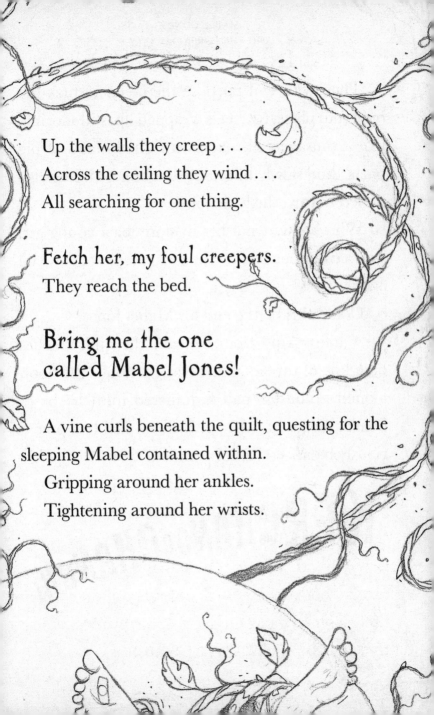

Up the walls they creep . . .
Across the ceiling they wind . . .
All searching for one thing.

Fetch her, my foul creepers.
They reach the bed.

Bring me the one called Mabel Jones!

A vine curls beneath the quilt, questing for the sleeping Mabel contained within.
Gripping around her ankles.
Tightening around her wrists.

Then with evil purpose the creepers tuck the quilt into place. Mabel is wrapped up, still snoring, like a sausage roll made with girl instead of pig parts. And slowly but surely the bundled snuglet is pulled toward the wardrobe.

Who knows what lies in store for a young girl stolen from her bed by the foul creepers of an evil enchantress?

Could this be the end for Mabel Jones?

A toe poking from beneath the quilt catches on a line of thread stretched tight above the floor, looped around a nail hammered into the base-board, then stretched upward and tied to a precariously balanced can of pennies.

KERCHANGaCHANG!!!

A booby trap! Set by clever, resource-

ful Mabel Jones. She has had some experience with unlikely adventures such as these. If you have been snatched from your bedroom once, then it pays to take great care it never happens again.

Mabel Jones was woken by a sudden noise.

She had been having a strange dream that she was being dragged into the wardrobe by the tendrils of an evil creeping vine. Then she realized it wasn't a nightmare.

It was **really happening**.

She opened her mouth to scream, but a thick vine covered her face, smothering her cry for help. Mabel, a skilled vegetarian, bit down hard and tore off a fleshy chunk of plant with her teeth.

Vile and bitter sap filled her mouth, like she had just swigged on a bottle of nit lotion. The bitten vine recoiled, spilling sap on the bedroom carpet.

Mabel bit another vine and her arm was free.

Free enough to grab a nearby shoe and use it to hammer at the vines that dragged her toward the wardrobe. Vine by vine she fought the plant, until she was sitting in a pool of mushed and mangled stems. The creepers were retreating now, shrinking back into the wardrobe. The spell was broken.

Mabel sat panting in the remains of her bedroom.

My name is Mabel Jones, and I am not scared of anything.

But something is wrong, Mabel.

Something precious is missing.

Something very precious indeed.

"My matchbox full of toenail clippings!"

Four years' work—gone.

And something else, Mabel?

"Oh, and the crib is empty."

MAGGIE IS GONE!

Mabel's sister, sleeping soundly, stood no chance. Plucked from her crib and dragged into the wardrobe, along with a Tupperware box of Legos, Mabel's recorder, and, of course, the toenail-clipping collection.

Look!

The final vine is disappearing back into the wardrobe! Mabel leaps to stop it. Maggie Jones may well be a slightly inconvenient and annoying baby sister, but she is *Mabel's* slightly inconvenient and annoying baby sister.

She grabs the vine and for a moment she holds it fast.

"GIVE. ME. BACK. MY. SISTER!"

Then the vine tugs, sudden and swift, and Mabel falls forward into the wardrobe—into a hot, steaming mist, her fingers still gripped around the end of the tendril.

Somewhere in the distance, the familiar sound of a wailing baby can be heard.

MAGGIE!

Then the vine snaps, weakened by the earlier bites of the desperate Mabel Jones.

And she is fal ling . . .